Hard Ever After

By Laura Kaye

Hard Ever After

A HARD INK NOVELLA

LAURA KAYE

AVONIMPULSE
An Imprint of HarperCollinsPublishers

Excerpt from *Ride Hard* copyright © 2016 by Laura Kaye.
Excerpt from *Everything She Wanted* copyright © 2016 by Jennifer Ryan.
Excerpt from *When We Kiss* copyright © 2016 by Darcy Burke.

EPub Edition FEBRUARY 2016 ISBN: 9780062421722

Print Edition ISBN: 9780062421746

Avon, Avon Impulse, and the Avon Impulse logo are trademarks of HarperCollins Publishers.

10 9 8 7 6 5 4 3

Dear Readers,
This book is my love letter to you.
Read hard, always and forever,
LK

Chapter One

"I DON'T WANT to let you go," Nick Rixey said, lying on his back in bed with Becca Merritt sprawled half on top of him. Dawn was already around the corner, but neither of them had slept much. At least he wasn't the only one who was a little stressed out about life returning to normal. You'd think it would be the opposite. But it's funny how your body and brain could get used to operating in crisis mode—and resist the reality that the crisis was over.

Becca traced a ticklish pattern across his chest with her fingertips. "I'm just going to work," she said. "I've been off for two months. It's time."

"I know," he said, pressing a kiss to her soft blond waves.

"But we might have time for a proper good-bye before I have to go," she said, a smile plain in her voice.

Nick couldn't help but grin, and Becca was a big part of why that was so much easier to do these days. "Might

we now? And what would a proper good-bye look like?"
Against his belly, his cock hardened.

"Mmm, a back rub might be nice," she said, her tone full of teasing.

"That's all?" He reached down to stroke his cock, and her head shifted, following the movement. And fuck if her watching him jack himself didn't get him even hotter. How the hell was he supposed to let her out of his sight for a twelve-hour shift at the hospital after they'd been around each other twenty-four/seven for most of the last two months?

"Maybe this, too." Becca slid down his body and joined her hand with his. Her tongue swirled around the head of his cock and her lips sucked at the tip as their hands moved together.

"Fuck, Sunshine. Take all of me," Nick rasped.

She pushed onto her knees, her face so filled with desire—for him—that it blew his mind. Every damn time. Looking him in the eye with those pretty baby blues, she leaned over and swallowed his length inch by maddening inch until he was buried in the back of her throat.

His hand went to her hair and his hips surged. "God, yes." For a few long moments, he savored the pleasure she was pulling out of his body with her lips and tongue and hands. And then he cupped her cheek in his palm. "Lay down," he said.

Smiling at him, Becca stretched out on her belly and laid her head on folded hands. Nick straddled her upper thighs, his cock rubbing against her ass as he smoothed his palms over her beautiful golden skin. To think that for most of the past year he'd been lonely, purposeless, angry, battling with demons so numerous it was hard to believe that they'd mostly been slayed. And it was Becca's walking through the door of his tattoo shop that had put him on the road to getting justice, having his honor restored, and clearing his name—not to mention finding love.

Becca Merritt had saved his life in every way that mattered.

Because of her, he had purpose again in a new business. His surviving Army Special Forces teammates—his family by choice if not by blood—were back working and fighting at his side. And he had hope for the future in a way he hadn't in a very long time, not since a roadside ambush in Afghanistan had killed half his team, sullied the name of his mentor and commander, and ended in the other-than-honorable discharge of Nick and his team. Not to mention injuring him and two of the other survivors. Although, shit, they'd all walked away with soul-deep wounds even if they hadn't been visible to the eye.

But that was all behind them now. After weeks of investigations, fighting, and off-the-books operations against a shit-ton of enemies, he and his team had come out on top and the bad guys were either dead or in custody. And now Nick could see the future stretching out in front of him. And this woman was at the very center of his vision.

"How's that feel?" he asked, kneading at Becca's shoulders. The position tugged at the lingering injuries he bore in his hip and lower back, where he'd taken two rounds during the ambush, but fuck if he was letting his body ruin this perfect moment of peace and closeness between them.

"Really good," she whispered.

He worked his way down her spine in a series of slow, deep massages. When he got to her ass, he pressed his cock between her cheeks and slowly stroked himself against her. Becca moaned. And Nick couldn't wait anymore. He had to get in her. "You wet for me, Sunshine?" He slipped his fingers between her legs and found her hot and slick and more than ready. "Aw, fuck, yeah you are."

"Always wet for you," she said, arching her back.

Straddling her thighs, Nick penetrated her, both of them moaning as he slid home.

"Oh, God, Nick," Becca rasped.

Grasping her cheeks, he began to move, his eyes trained on where he disappeared inside her. "So good together. Every damn time."

"Yes," she said, arching into him, urging him faster, harder.

Nick braced his arms against the bed and gave her everything he had—his body, his heart, his soul. The sounds of panting breaths and pleasured moans and slapping skin filled the gray-lit room. "Touch yourself," he said. "I want you to come on me."

Becca slid a hand between her legs, and Nick closed every bit of distance between them, his body coming down and covering her from head to toes. He wrapped one arm around her shoulder and another around her head, his fingers tangling in all that beautiful, soft blond hair. "Love you so fucking much," he rasped into her ear.

"Nick," she whispered, her tone tortured and needy. Her movements grew jerky and desperate beneath him, and then she was moaning and coming, her body fisting around him and stealing his sanity.

"Aw, God, Becca," he groaned as his orgasm nailed him in the back. On a series of punctuated thrusts, he sought to get as deep as he could as he poured himself into her.

When their bodies calmed, Nick shifted, but Becca grasped at his hip. "Don't leave yet."

"Don't want to crush you," he said, kissing her temple.

"I like the feeling of you on top of me."

Nick chuffed out a small laugh. "Keep talking like that, and I'm gonna get hard again."

Becca smiled. "I wouldn't complain."

His head resting against hers, Nick sighed. Contentment. Such a foreign feeling. And yet he found it in Becca's arms. And had, from the very beginning, even when he'd been too stubborn and too proud to see everything that she was.

And that was the moment Nick knew what he was doing during Becca's first day back to work. He wanted her in his life. He wanted that life to start now. Hell, to start yesterday. And he wanted it to be forever.

And that meant he needed a ring. The rightness of the idea settled bone-deep inside him. As much as anyone, he knew how life could change in a single unexpected instant. No way did he want to wait even a second more for their future to start.

"Nick?" she said, pulling him from the plans taking shape in his head.

"Yeah?"

"Will you do something for me tonight?"

He finally shifted off her, his body settling alongside hers so he could look at her while they talked. "You can always assume the answer to that will be yes, Sunshine," he said, brushing her hair back off her face.

"I've been thinking about it, and I'd like you to give me a tattoo tonight," she said, bright blue eyes looking up at him with so much warmth.

The request sent his heart beating a little faster. Nick was half owner of Hard Ink Tattoo, though he'd only been working as a tattoo artist on a part-time basis since he'd been discharged from the Army. "You know I've been dying to put my ink on you," he said with a smile.

She grinned. "Well, now's your chance." She pointed toward the drawer on the nightstand. "I printed something out to give you an idea."

Nick couldn't move fast enough. After all the times they'd talked about what she'd want if she ever got a tattoo, and after all the times he'd drawn on her body with skin markers just to put his mark on her—even if only temporarily—he couldn't wait to see what she'd finally decided she wanted on her skin. Forever. He sat on the edge of the bed and unfolded the sheet while Becca knelt behind him, her front pressed tight to his back, her arms wrapped around his stomach.

It was three intertwined cursive words.

Only. Always. Forever.

"Fuck, Sunshine," Nick said, remembering the night he'd shown her the tattoo he'd gotten on his forearm for her and she'd written the word *YOURS* over her heart with a marker. That had set off a raw, urgent lovemaking that had included them writing words of claiming and love and intention all over each other.

Only. Always. Forever.

"What do you think?" she asked.

"I think it's perfect," Nick said, staring at the page. Damn if his throat didn't get a little tight at the thought that she wanted to put their words on her body. "Do you know where you want it?"

She kissed the side of his neck and her breath caressed his ear. "On my right shoulder."

Nodding, Nick could already picture it—and it made him even more certain about what he needed to do today. "It'll look beautiful there, Becca." He shifted to the side so he could wrap her in his arms. "You make me fall in love with you a little more every day. You know that?"

"I think that's the sweetest thing anyone's ever said to me." Her kiss was slow and sweet and lingering. "I don't want to, but I should get moving."

"I know," Nick said, standing and giving her a hand off the bed. He watched her walk into the bathroom, his mind back on his plan for the day. Because he was giving her more than a tattoo tonight. And he couldn't fucking wait.

Chapter Two

A FEW BLOCKS away from the hospital, the nerves Becca had been shoving down all morning finally pushed through. Ridiculous to be nervous about returning to a place where she'd worked for years. But she was. Because the last time she'd been there, a man named Tyrell Woodson had grabbed her from behind, jabbed a knife into her ribs, and tried to abduct her from the staff lounge. Only her struggling—getting cut in the process—and Nick arriving, well, in the nick of time, had saved her from God only knew what horrible fate.

Even worse? The man had gotten away and tried to grab her again, though the team had caught him that time and made sure he wouldn't be a problem anymore. So Becca shouldn't be nervous. She shouldn't be worrying. And she certainly didn't want to let on to Nick that she was.

They caught the red light a block away from the hospital's downtown Baltimore campus, and Nick turned to her from the driver's seat. "I'll pick you up at seven, and then we can grab some dinner and head down to Hard Ink."

"Sounds like a plan," she said with a smile, looking forward so much to finally getting a tattoo—from Nick. He brought their joined hands to his mouth and kissed her knuckles. God, she loved this man. He'd insisted on driving her. Truth be told, she hadn't minded the extra time with him. It was going to be weird to go back to work in the emergency department after all these months off. All the people at Hard Ink had come to feel like her family now in addition to her brother, Charlie, who was in a relationship with Nick's younger brother, Jeremy. She was going to miss seeing them all the time.

Moments later, Nick pulled the car over to the curb in front of the hospital. "Have a great day, Sunshine," he said, leaning over the center console. His kisses made her want to stay. "Be safe."

"I will," she said, ignoring the butterflies in her belly. It really was ridiculous. "Miss you already." And then she was pushing out of the car and crossing the wide sidewalk plaza in front of the hospital's tall glass entrance. She'd purposely arrived close to the beginning of her shift so that she wouldn't have much time before she'd be busy, which she knew would be the perfect cure for her nerves.

A chorus of greetings rose up from the nurse's station of the emergency department. Becca made her way inside and gave a round of hugs. Luckily, things were busy enough with the shift change that no one had time to linger. She headed to the staff lounge to stow her belongings.

Alison Harding came out of the lounge just as Becca reached for the door. "Oh, Becca, it's so good to have you back," the woman said, a hint of sadness in her bright green eyes. Becca had been subbing for Alison the day the attempted abduction had occurred, and Alison had sent more than one guilt-ridden, apologetic text. Not that Becca blamed her. It was hardly Alison's fault that the undercover military investigation into narcotics smuggling that Becca's father had been investigating in Afghanistan had spilled over into the United States. Or that the bad guys had been selling their heroin to the Church Gang, headquartered just across the city in Baltimore. Or that somehow the bad guys had discovered that Charlie had stumbled onto his father's activities, leading them to grab him and attempt to grab Becca as well.

"It's good to be back," Becca said.

"How are you doing? Did the police ever catch the guy?" Alison asked, tucking a strand of light brown hair behind her ear.

"No, they didn't," Becca said, unable to share what she did know—that Nick's team had caught and interrogated Woodson, and that Nick had threatened the man within an inch of his life. "But I'm good. Really good."

Alison frowned. "God, it's scary that he's still out there, isn't it?"

Becca's belly did a little flip. "No, I really think he's long gone," she said. Marz had taken video of him spilling his guts about the Church Gang's secrets, which Nick had promised to put in the gang leader's hands should Woodson ever come near Becca again. Already beaten up for having failed to capture Becca, Woodson had tripped all over himself promising to stay away for good.

"Well, I hope so." Alison gave her an unconvincing smile. "All right. I'll see you out there." She squeezed Becca's arm and headed down the hall.

Taking a deep breath, Becca pushed into the room where she'd been attacked, worried that it was going to be filled with all kinds of ghosts. Instead, she found a big bouquet of balloons, a sheet cake that read, *Welcome back, Becca!* and a plastic-wrapped bunch of flowers lying on one of the tables. The overhead lights and morning sunshine spilling through the window near the door— the door through which Woodson had tried to drag her—made the room bright and cheery, not the scary, dark place her nightmares sometimes depicted.

Shaking her head at herself, Becca crossed to her locker and ditched her purse. She made a small corner piece of cake with a big pink frosting flower her breakfast, then found herself so immersed in patients that it was noon before she knew it—and time for the other thing she wasn't looking forward to: an appointment with a hospital psychologist. It was standard operating procedure after the attack and the long leave of absence, but Becca wasn't relishing being asked to talk about what had happened. And she was well aware that medical personnel sometimes made the worst patients, herself included. She was way more comfortable taking care of others than being taken care of herself.

She waited in the fifth-floor mental health services suite. Finally, the door to the waiting room opened, and a tall, attractive woman in dress pants and a crisp blouse stepped out. "Becca Merritt?"

"Yes," Becca said, tossing the magazine she'd been skimming to the coffee table.

"I'm Dr. Parker," the woman said. "Please, come in."

Becca had seen her around the hospital a few times but didn't know her well. "Thanks," she said, slipping into the well-appointed office—all warm tones and relaxing landscape prints. She took a seat on the sofa.

The doctor grabbed a pen and folder from her desk, then sat in an armchair and smiled at Becca. "How has your first day back to work been?"

"Fine. Busy. But I'm right back in the swing of things," Becca said, lacing her fingers in her lap.

"Good, I'm glad to hear it. You know this meeting is routine. The hospital just needs to touch base, given the traumatic event that led to your leave of absence." Dr. Parker scanned a sheet inside Becca's folder.

Becca nodded. "I understand." Woodson had somehow managed to gain access to a set of hospital credentials and had posed as a maintenance man, so the hospital had been concerned that Becca would sue. But more than that, traumatic events could lead to bad decision making, which was never an acceptable risk when those decisions were of the life-and-death variety.

"So how are you doing? How are you finding being back in the hospital again?" The doctor's expression was carefully neutral, but Becca didn't doubt for a moment that her reactions were being scrutinized.

So she went for honesty. "I was a little nervous about coming in before I got here this morning, but once I was here, I was fine. As soon as the shift started, everything felt normal. So I think I'm doing pretty good."

Dr. Parker nodded. "I'm glad to hear it. Are you having any nightmares, anxiety, issues with panic, sleep or appetite problems?"

Becca clutched her hands tighter. "I've had occasional nightmares, and for a while I was jumpy if someone approached me from behind, but I haven't had any of the other issues." Frankly, given everything that Nick's team had faced during their investigation into the men who'd killed her father and abducted Charlie, Becca's issues had taken a total backseat. And she'd been fine with that. Because she *had been* fine. And the last thing she'd wanted to do was distract or worry Nick by making him think she was anything but fine. Not when his life had been on the line—so many times. "The whole thing could've turned out a lot worse than it did, so I mostly feel lucky."

"That's a great way to look at it." The doctor scribbled something inside the folder. "Do you have any concerns about being back to work?"

"None," Becca said. "I'm glad to be back." And she was. She'd known she wanted to be a nurse since the age of thirteen, when her mother had died of an aneurysm. The feeling of helplessness Becca had experienced that night had made her determined to be able to help if something similar ever happened again to someone she cared about. She loved what she did.

After a few more questions, Dr. Parker handed her a form. "I'm happy to clear you to return," she said. "Just sign where it's highlighted."

"Great," Becca said. "Thank you." She signed and handed back the form, and then it was time for her lunch break.

Back in the staff lounge, she found a couple of people hanging out around the half-demolished cake. She was glad for the company and conversation as she settled down to the turkey sandwich, chips, and yogurt she'd brought from home, and she was equally glad to find that no one treated her weirdly despite the fact that everyone knew what had happened to her that day. Even if you could keep gossip that juicy under wraps around there, which you couldn't, the hospital had undertaken a security reevaluation and had implemented some new procedures and security mechanisms as a result. So her attack was no secret whatsoever.

Still, as the day progressed and patients were admitted in a nonstop stream, she found it easier and easier to relax. Finally, seven o'clock rolled around, and a bundle of anticipation took root in her belly. She couldn't wait to see Nick, and she really couldn't wait for him to do her first tattoo.

In the staff lounge, she collected her purse from her locker and gathered the flowers to take home. There wasn't much cake left, and she figured the night shift would easily finish it. The balloons made the otherwise plain blue-and-white lounge more cheery, so she decided to leave them there. They wouldn't fit in Nick's sports car anyway.

Not wanting to keep Nick waiting, Becca rushed across the room with her arms full. The door yanked open right in front of her, and a tall, bald man with dark brown skin stepped into the opening, looming over her.

Becca nearly choked on a gasp. Tyrell Woodson. For a moment, she was sucked back into the past so thoroughly that everything around her disappeared.

"Oh, sorry about that," the man said, his voice deep and friendly.

She blinked and swallowed hard. *Not Woodson. Holy shit, not Woodson. What's wrong with me?* Becca forced a smile. "Oh, no. Not your fault," she managed. "I wasn't paying attention." He wore blue scrubs, not a maintenance uniform. And the identification tag clipped to his pocket read *Benton Tucker, Certified Nursing Assistant.* She stepped back to let him in.

He pointed at the flowers. "Are you Becca?"

"Uh, yeah," she said, her heart still racing in her chest. "How'd you know?"

"The cake. I had a piece earlier. When it still said your name," he said with a deep chuckle.

She smiled. "Right. Glad you got some, because it's almost gone. Free food never lasts long."

Another chuckle. "I guess that's right. I'm Ben," he said, extending his hand. "I've only been here for about a month."

"Nice to meet you, Ben," she said, returning the shake

and feeling bad for the way she'd reacted to him, which had been not only ridiculous but also embarrassing. Not to mention a little concerning. For a moment, her brain had been entirely convinced that Woodson had been standing in front of her, despite the fact that Ben bore only a superficial resemblance to him. While both men were tall and dark skinned, Ben's head wasn't bald, like Woodson's, but was covered with closely trimmed hair. Ben didn't have any tattoos or scars, whereas Woodson had been covered in them. Ben's face was lean, and he wore a neatly trimmed goatee, where Woodson's face had been round, his cheeks full. And Ben radiated an easygoing good humor, not the menace she'd gotten from Woodson. "Well, hopefully our shifts will overlap soon. Hope you have a good night."

"You, too, Becca." He gave a wave and turned for the cake table.

Becca pushed out into the hall. After she'd successfully battled back her nerves all day, freaking out just because a man had stepped in front of her made her feel defeated and weak and stupid. And that pissed her off. She was stronger than this. And she refused to let a little anxiety get the better of her. Woodson was gone. The Church Gang had been largely destroyed. And Nick and his team had exposed the corruption that had led to her father's death and the team's being railroaded out of the Army. They'd also gotten the justice they deserved.

Everything was good now. The crises were all behind them.

Outside, July heat wrapped around her despite the

evening hour, but the only thing Becca cared about was the man sitting in the black car idling at the curb. She rushed across the plaza, the smile on her face growing when Nick noticed her coming.

She couldn't get in the car fast enough. "Hi," she said.

"Sunshine," Nick said, the word filled with so much emotion it made tears prickle against the backs of her eyes. "Missed you." His hand found the back of her neck and pulled her in for a long kiss.

"Missed you, too," she said. His presence chased away the last of her nerves and allowed her to take a deep, cleansing breath. She was fine. No big deal.

He threw the car into gear and eased into traffic. "So, how was your day? Everything go okay?"

"Yeah," Becca said. "Everything went great."

"YOU MADE SLOPPY JOES," Becca said with a big grin when they got home. The rich, spicy smell of Nick's one and only specialty filled the whole loft apartment—and the gesture filled her heart with so much affection. He'd made her Sloppy Joes the very first night she'd spent there at Hard Ink, back when everything had seemed so uncertain, back when it had seemed like she might lose everyone she had left.

Nick grinned as he moved to the Crock-Pot on the counter and lifted the lid. "I did. Thought you might enjoy something homemade after a long shift."

Becca came up behind him and wrapped her arms around his firm stomach. "You're the sweetest."

He chuckled as he stirred the thick, meaty sauce. "Don't tell anyone."

"Too late," Jeremy said as he walked into the room, Charlie right behind him. The two of them were pretty much attached at the hip these days, which Becca found completely awesome. Her brother had been a loner for so much of his life. He deserved someone as special and fun and loving as Jeremy Rixey.

Eileen loped out after them. Becca had rescued the three-legged German shepherd puppy off the street near the hospital the first week she'd met Nick, back before she'd realized she'd never be returning to her own place again. At first, that was because it hadn't been safe—multiple break-ins had proven that. Now, even though all their mysteries had been solved and threats had been neutralized, it was because her home was here.

"Hey," Becca said, bending down to pet the monster-sized puppy. "You guys are just in time. We're getting ready to eat. Wanna join?"

Jeremy ran his inked hand over his short dark-brown hair, which was still growing out following brain surgery just over a month ago. None of them had emerged unscathed from the investigation into the corruption that had killed her father and blackened his team's reputations. Charlie had been abducted and maimed, two of his fingers cut off to try to make him talk. And Jeremy had been pistol-whipped by a fleeing bad guy who'd attacked them at a funeral. But both of them were doing so much better now. "We already had some," Jeremy said with a grin. "You know I wouldn't miss Nick's Sloppy Joes."

"Pretty much everyone else ate already," Nick said, pressing a kiss against Becca's hair. "Everyone" meaning the other four members of Nick's team and their respective girlfriends, all of whom were crashing in temporary digs here until a huge-scale rebuilding and renovation project was done, which would create six loft-style apartments in the other half of the L-shaped Hard Ink building.

Peering out from between long strands of blond hair, Charlie nodded. "We're gonna catch a movie."

After weeks of being on lockdown here, the idea of just going out to do something as casual and normal as seeing a movie still felt strange to Becca. "Oh, well, that sounds like fun."

"How was work today?" Charlie asked in that quiet way he had.

She came around the counter to him. Sometimes she was completely overwhelmed by her relief that they'd managed to rescue him from the Church Gang. And by her love for him, her only remaining family member. "It was good. Business as usual." Playfully, she pushed his hair back off his face. "I like it long, you know."

"Yeah?" he asked, his gaze a little shy. Even around her. "Me too."

"Me too," Jeremy said in a loaded tone, waggling his eyebrows as he planted a kiss on Charlie's cheek.

Becca laughed and held up her hands as Charlie's cheeks pinked, which was when she noticed the guys' T-shirts. Jeremy's was white with a headless stick figure. It read, *I need head.* Charlie's was blue and read, *I'm Getting Real Tired of Wearing Pants and Having Responsibilities.* Jeremy's innuendo-filled T-shirt collection was legendary around here, and Charlie had been borrowing Jer's clothes ever since he'd been rescued, although he usually picked the least dirty shirts Jeremy had. It was just another thing Becca loved about Jeremy, and about the way he loved and took care of her brother.

"Speaking of responsibilities, how did things go with the construction today?" she asked as Nick passed her two plates. She placed them on the breakfast bar, then grabbed some silverware and napkins.

Jeremy flicked his tongue against the piercing on his bottom lip and braced his hands on the counter. "Inspectors were out this morning and signed off on everything that's been done so far. Contractor's hoping to have the exterior shell totally done before winter. Fingers crossed."

"Considering a few weeks ago there was just a big hole out there, that sounds pretty good," Becca said.

"Yeah," Jeremy said, something dark momentarily passing through his gaze. And Becca didn't have to guess at what it was. There'd been a big hole because the arm of the building that had previously stood in that spot had been destroyed by a military-grade explosive device launched at the building in a predawn attack by the enemies of Nick's team. An attack that had resulted in the deaths of two of Jeremy's friends, members of the Raven Riders Motorcycle Club, which had been helping protect them. On some level, Becca knew Jeremy blamed himself for that. "Well, we better go."

Charlie nodded and made for the door, where he paused for a moment. "Hey, Becca?"

"Yeah?"

For a moment it seemed like he struggled for words. "Have a good night," he finally said, and then he ducked out, Jeremy right behind him.

"Thanks," she said, then turned to Nick. "Was that weird, or is it just me?"

Nick shrugged as he pulled buns out of a bag. "I think he was worried about you being at work today."

"Oh." The thought made her heart squeeze.

Soon, she and Nick were seated at the bar together with overflowing Sloppy Joe sandwiches, some of the pasta salad she'd made over the weekend, and chips. Eileen curled up on the floor next to Becca's tall chair.

"This is the best dinner ever," she said.

"That's because you're easy to please," he said with a smile that brought his dimple out to play. A man with so many rough edges . . . and a dimple. It slayed her every time.

"So how was your day?" she asked.

"Uh, good. Made a lot of progress on the new office," he said. They were turning the previously empty first-floor spot next to their tattoo shop into a high-tech suite of offices for the new security consulting company Nick and his team were opening. "Kinda funny that Jeremy bought this old warehouse because it was cheap, and now it's turned out to be the perfect space for all of us."

Becca smiled. "Yeah. I'm glad everyone is still going to be around here when all the work is done." It had seemed so empty around the building when, earlier in the summer, most of the team had cleared out to return to their homes and pack up their lives to relocate here permanently.

"Me too, Sunshine. This all feels right." Nick wiped up some sauce from his plate with the edge of his bun.

"Where is everyone anyway?" Becca asked. "It's so

quiet." With six couples living out of two loft apartments, only one of which had a finished kitchen, it often felt a little like a college dorm around there.

"Shane, Sara, Easy, and Jenna went out to dinner earlier. And I think Beckett, Kat, Marz, and Emilie decided to finish up some painting downstairs."

Becca leaned in for a kiss. "It's weird to be alone."

Nick laughed. "Roger that."

"We could have sex on the counter," Becca said, giving him a seductive look.

He froze with a potato chip halfway to his mouth. "Is this something you've been thinking about?"

"Pretty much if it involves you and sex, you can bet I've thought about it," Becca said, grinning at the expression on his face, part dumbfounded, part aroused. "What can I say? You're very inspiring."

He wiped his mouth and slipped off his stool, then he spun her around to face him, his big body surrounding hers. He tilted up her chin. "Right back atcha, Becca. But nothing is sidetracking me from getting my ink on you tonight. You hear me?"

She rested her hands against his chest. "No sidetracking intended."

His fingers slid into her hair. "Uh-huh. Now, you ready for your tattoo? Because I'm dying to get my hands on you."

WEARING ONLY HER bra and jeans, Becca sat in a chair in the middle of Nick's tattoo room. Since the shop was closed while Jeremy focused on getting the construction on the other half of the building started, they were the only ones down there. The driving beat of a rock song played from the radio as Nick moved around the room getting everything ready.

Cabinets and a long counter filled one wall, which was otherwise decorated with drawings, tattoo designs, posters, and photographs of clients.

Becca had seen Nick work before and loved the dichotomy of this hard-edged, lethal soldier having a soft, artistic side. He was really freaking talented, too.

He handed her three sheets of paper. "I worked up a couple different fonts. What do you think?"

She shifted between the pages. "This one," she said, settling on the cursive design that best interweaved the letters in the words *Only, Always, Forever.*

"That was my favorite, too," he said, giving her a wink. "How is this for size? Bigger? Smaller?"

The total design as he had it on the sheet was about four inches square, the words stacked atop one another. "This looks good to me. What do you think?"

Nick nodded and came behind her. He folded the sheet to focus on the design, then held it against the back of her right shoulder. "Yeah. This is a good size for the space. Gonna be fucking beautiful." He leaned down and pressed a kiss to her skin. "Let me go make the stencil, and we're ready to go."

A few minutes later, he cleaned her skin, affixed the stencil, and let her look at its placement before getting her settled into the chair again.

He pulled her bra strap off to the side. "Ready?"

"Very," she said, butterflies doing a small loop in her belly.

The tattoo machine came to life on a low buzz. "Just relax and let me know if you need a break, okay?" he said, dipping the tip into a little plastic cup of black ink.

"Okay." His gloved hands fell against her skin, and then the needles. Almost a scratching feeling, it didn't hurt nearly as bad as she thought it would. And just like when he'd drawn on her with skin markers, she was already dying to see what it looked like.

"How you doing?" he asked in a voice full of concentration she found utterly sexy. Just the thought that he was permanently altering her skin—just like he'd permanently altered her heart, her life, her very soul—sent a hot thrill through her blood.

"I'm good," she said, relaxing into the sensation of the bite moving across her skin. "Is it weird that I kinda like how it feels?"

He didn't answer right away as the needle moved in a long line. He pulled the machine away and wiped at her shoulder. "Not weird at all," he said, his voice a little gravelly. "Some people like the sensation and even find getting tattoos addictive."

"I can see that," she said. He worked without talking for a stretch, and the combination of the quiet intensity radiating off of him, the driving rock beat, and the buzz of the machine was heady and intoxicating. She found herself breathing a little faster and wanting so much more of him to be touching so much more of her. If she thought he was sexy putting ink on someone else, it was nothing compared to how she felt when he was doing it to her.

"What are you thinking about so hard?" Nick asked, his breath caressing her bare shoulder.

"Really want to know?" she asked, already smiling at what his reaction might be.

"Always," he said, wiping at her skin. He dipped the machine in the ink and leaned in again.

"How turned on this is making me." She really wanted to turn to see his expression but knew she wasn't supposed to move.

He pulled the machine away again. "Jesus, Becca. You're killing me here."

She grinned. "I asked if you really wanted to know."

Nick chuffed out a laugh. "Yeah, well, I've never had a fucking hard-on the entire time I've done a tattoo before, so you're not the only one."

Becca unleashed a small moan. "Now you've got me thinking about your cock, Nick." She couldn't help the hint of a whine in her voice.

"You'll never convince me that that's a bad thing, Sunshine."

"God, I really want to touch you right now," she said, heat spreading over her body.

"Be still," he said, his tone full of a stern command that made her smile.

"Yes, sir."

"Fucking *yes, sir*," he grumbled under his breath.

Another long stretch passed without them talking,

but knowing that what they were doing was arousing Nick as much as it was her made her wet and needy and absolutely ready to jump him the minute she could.

Nearly ninety minutes had passed by the time Nick said, "There. It's done." He wiped at her skin and handed her a mirror. "Take a look."

Anticipation made her belly feel like she was looking over the edge of a tall cliff. She crossed to the mirror and turned her back to it, then lifted the hand mirror to see her first tattoo.

"Oh, Nick," she said, her gaze drinking it in. The way the stacked letters intertwined with one another was so beautifully done. "It's . . . gorgeous." Her heart squeezed in her chest. "You are so freaking talented." She looked from the mirror to where he still sat, his gaze glued to her face.

"I think it looks phenomenal on you. You really like it?" he asked.

She looked at her ink again. The stark crispness of the black lettering was so striking against her skin. She adored everything about it—the design, the words, their meaning. "I don't just like it. I love it, Nick. It's perfect. Everything I wanted." Her gaze cut back to him. "Just like you."

"Come here," he said, his voice a little rough. When she stood right in front of him, he pressed a kiss between her breasts. "It was an honor, you letting me do that."

She dragged her hands through his dark brown hair. "Sweet, sweet man," she said, leaning down to kiss him. It started off soft, full of gratitude and love, but quickly flashed hot until they were devouring one another, claiming, wanting, moaning.

"Fuck, Becca," he said, pulling back. "Let me take care of your tattoo."

Wiping the wetness from her lips, she smiled and nodded. "Okay." She sat back in the chair, and Nick cleaned the skin over her tattoo and taped a bandage to it.

"All done," he said. "Now, there's just one more thing I need to do."

Chapter Four

HOLY HELL, HAD Nick ever been this nervous in his life? He'd faced down warlords, captured terrorists, survived IED explosions, and been shot on multiple occasions. Yet he'd never felt the kind of queasy, can't-quite-manage-a-deep-breath nerves he felt just then.

He retrieved the little black box from the drawer where he'd hidden it, fisted it in his palm, and came to stand in front of Becca. He gave her a hand to stand up, then slowly sank to one knee.

"What are you—" Becca gasped. "Nick?"

"Becca." Looking up at her beautiful face, he grasped her left hand. "When you walked through my door, you changed my whole life. You gave me purpose when I had none. You brought my family back together when I was so alone. You believed in me when no one else did, including myself. You fought for me and loved me and made me a better man." Glassy, bright blue eyes stared down at him with so much love. "You shined light on places inside me I thought would never emerge from the dark, and you helped me reclaim my integrity, my honor, and my life." A knot lodged in Nick's throat. "You saved me from becoming someone I didn't recognize, and because of you I have a life worth living. But only if you'll walk it with me."

"Nick," she rasped, her voice thick with unshed tears.

He flipped open the box and pulled out the diamond and platinum round-cut ring. A halo of smaller stones surrounded the center stone, creating what to him looked like a sun. More accent stones lined the band, giving it a classic, vintage look. He'd known it was the right ring as soon as he'd seen it. Slowly, he slid the diamond onto Becca's ring finger. "I love you with everything that I am, and everything I want to be. Please do me the greatest honor of my life and say you'll be my wife, my partner, my best friend, my companion. Becca Merritt, will you marry me?"

For a split second that felt like eternity, she looked down at her shaking hand. And then she sank to her knees in front of him and grasped his face. "Yes," she said, kissing him. "Only you. Always you. Forever you, Nick. Yes."

"Aw, Sunshine," he said, sliding his hands into her hair. "You make me happier than I ever thought I could be."

"I feel the exact same way," she said, tears finally leaking from the corners of her eyes. "I love you so much."

He kissed her on a groan, his spirit more buoyant and triumphant than it had ever been. Even more than when their records had been cleared and their honor had been restored. That had been exactly what he'd deserved, but this . . . this was more than he ever knew to want.

Becca's hands fisted in his shirt as she sucked hard on his tongue, a needy, desperate moan spilling from her throat. The sound shot right to his cock, making him rock hard in an instant and bringing back every bit of the aching lust he'd felt while he'd been doing her tattoo. Christ, if he thought it was arousing to mark her with his ink, it was nothing compared to what it did to him to know she'd just agreed to be his forever. He was fucking flying.

Nick tore open the button to her jeans. "Need in you."

"Yes," she said, tugging up his shirt. He helped her pull it over his head. For a moment, they were a whirl of shedding clothes and grasping hands and claiming kisses until they were both naked and panting and hot.

He sat in the chair where she'd been sitting and guided her down to his lap, her back to his front. "Take me inside of you, Becca. Ride me so fucking hard."

She took his cock in hand and sank down on him in one slow, slick stroke. "Oh, God," she rasped when he bottomed out inside her. "Needed you so much. All day."

He grasped her hips, his fingers digging into her soft flesh. "I'm here. Right here."

Hands braced on his thighs, Becca lifted herself up and down on his cock, riding him until they were both moaning, desperate, shaking. Her nails bit deliciously into his quads, making him do a double take at the big diamond on her left hand. And *fuck* if that didn't escalate the urgent ache in his balls—to pour himself deep, deep inside her, and never let go.

She threw her head back, sending her long blond waves cascading down his chest. He fisted a thick column of her hair in his hand, forcing her back further against him until she was reclined against his chest and impaled on his cock. "Want you to come all over me," he said, reaching around to stroke her. She arched on contact, but Nick held her fast against him as his fingers pressed firm, quick circles against her clit.

The diamond caught the light as she grasped and kneaded her breasts, her movements growing desperate as she thrust forward against his fingers and back against his cock. On a guttural moan, she held her breath and her core fisted around his length until her muscles were pulsing, sucking, squeezing the sanity from him. A high-pitched moan wrenched out of her as she went slack on his lap, and the languid satisfaction of her body made him feel ten feet tall.

"Holy shit," she rasped.

He smacked her ass. "Kneel on the chair and bend over."

"Ooh. Yes, sir," she said as he helped her stand. He grinned as she got into position and looked back over her shoulder.

Gut instinct had him pulling off the bandage covering her tattoo. "I wanna see this ink while I fuck you." He penetrated her inch by maddening inch, his gaze glued to the words she would wear forever. For him.

Gripping the back of the chair, she peered at the

design from the corner of her eye. "You're so good, Nick. All of you. I'm so lucky you're mine."

Her voice lit up places within him that once were so dark. Buried all the way inside her, he leaned over her back and braced his hand on the chair next to hers. Then his hips started to move in small, deep, punctuated thrusts that had her moaning with each stroke and his body screaming for release. As deep as it was, it wasn't deep enough. It would *never* be deep enough. "Fuck, Becca. Just want you so goddamned much."

"You have me, Nick. Oh, God," she rasped as he banded an arm around her ribs and moved faster. The chair screeched against the floor and their skin slapped against the percussive beat of a grinding rock song.

He clutched her left hand on the backrest of the chair, and the diamond bit into his palm. It was the nail in the coffin of his remaining reserve. On a shout, he buried himself balls deep and came until he couldn't help but rest his weight against Becca's back. When his body finally stilled, he wrapped both arms around her and pressed a soft, openmouthed kiss next to her tattoo. "I love you, Becca. And I always will."

NICK COULD BARELY keep the smile off his face as he opened the apartment door. Him, unable to hold back a smile. If that wasn't life doing a one-eighty, he didn't know what was.

"After you," he said to Becca. As she stepped inside the loft, he flicked on the lights to the main room.

"Surprise!" rang out in a great chorus of voices, along with a few barks. All their friends were there waiting for them—Jeremy and Charlie, Nick's sister, Kat, and all of Nick's teammates and their girlfriends. Baltimore police detective Kyler Vance, who'd been such an ally during their investigation, was there, too. And Nick had even managed to convince Walter and Louis Jackson to come. Walter had been Charlie's landlord and had taken a special interest in helping Becca, even calling in the assistance of his son, Louis, who'd turned out to be an amazing resource for the team as the coordinator of the city's task force on gangs.

"Oh, my God," Becca said with a huge smile on her face. She turned and threw her arms around Nick. "You planned all this?"

Now he could grin. "I did good, huh?"

She laughed and hugged him tighter. "You did amazing."

When they broke apart, he and Becca were surrounded by their friends and family, although the distinction didn't mean much in this room. These people were all their family of choice. Everyone offered words of congratulations as Becca showed off her ring and recounted his proposal.

"Congrats, man. I couldn't be happier for you," Jeremy said, wearing the most unreserved smile Nick had seen on his brother in weeks. Not that Nick could blame him—between recovering from brain surgery, managing the construction on the other half of the Hard Ink building, and grappling with the death of two friends in the attack, the guy had a lot on his plate.

"Thanks, Jeremy. That means a lot," Nick said. He

shook his brother's hand and tugged him in for a quick hug. "I'm happy for you, too. You and Charlie."

Becca arched a brow at Charlie. "So, going to a movie, huh?" Charlie's smile was a little sheepish, where Jer's was a total shit-eating number that said he was pleased with himself for pulling one over on her. "So you were in on all this?" she asked them.

Charlie nodded. "It's nice to have something else to celebrate."

"I couldn't agree more," Nick said as he watched Becca hug the blond-haired man who'd helped make tonight possible when he'd given Nick his blessing to propose to his sister.

Someone touched Nick's arm, and he turned to find Kat standing beside him. Short, with long brown hair, she matched Nick for stubbornness and guts, something she'd proven more than once during the recent investigation. "She's really good for you, Nick. You deserve this. And I'm really proud of you," Kat said. Given the way the two of them butted heads sometimes, the words meant a lot. They hugged, and Nick was reminded yet again just how much he had in his life now. Because of Becca.

"Thanks, Kat. Although all this happiness is really fucking weird," he said.

Rolling her bright green eyes, she shook her head. "Too damn bad. You'll just have to get used to it." She linked arms with Becca. "So when do we get to go dress shopping?"

"I'd love to help, too," Sara Dean said, brushing her red hair back from her face.

"I hadn't even thought about it yet," Becca said, looking between Kat and Sara. Of all the women here, Becca and Sara had known each other the longest. Nick knew that Becca held a special affection for Sara, who'd helped him and the team rescue Charlie from the basement of the strip club where Sara had been forced to work. "I'm off on Thursday and Friday, so maybe then? Jenna and Emilie can come, too. We'll do a whole girls' day."

"After everything that's happened, isn't it weird to think we can just go shopping?" Sara said. Words of agreement rose up all around, and Nick was glad that Becca had a close group of friends to share all this with.

Shane McCallan came up behind Sara and kissed her on the cheek. "Champagne?" He held out a tray of plastic flutes. Sara looked up at Shane with so much affection on her face, and Nick wondered if he and Becca were that blatant with their feelings. Hell, he guessed they probably were. But everyone in this room deserved a big old slice of happiness, so Nick couldn't begrudge a single one of them.

"You make a good waiter," Nick said to his best friend as he took a glass for Becca and himself. "In case this security business doesn't work out, and all."

"Don't make me tell you to fuck off at your engagement party," Shane said, a hint of his Southern accent coming through.

Nick laughed and shook the guy's free hand. "Thanks again for coming with me today."

"Wouldn't have been anywhere else," Shane said. And Nick knew that was true, despite the initial disbelief and subsequent ribbing Shane had dished out when Nick had told him what he planned to do.

When everyone had a glass of bubbly in their hands, Shane called out, "Hey everyone, gather 'round. I'd like to make a toast."

Standing in a big circle between the loft's open living room and kitchen, everyone quieted. Becca slipped her arm around Nick's back and leaned in tight against his side.

Shane held up his glass. "Nick Rixey is my best friend, my teammate, and my brother, and I know he'd lay down his life for me as quickly as I'd do the same for him."

"Fuckin' A," Nick said, giving Shane a nod. Their other teammates—Beckett Murda, Derek "Marz" Di-Marzio, and Edward "Easy" Cantrell—sent up words of support, too.

"So I couldn't be happier," Shane continued, "to see him getting everything he deserves. Well, maybe even more than he deserves, given how amazing Becca Merritt is."

Against a round of laughter, Nick grinned and nodded, while Becca protested and hugged him.

Shane winked at her. "Becca, you went above and beyond in helping us clear our names, and I will forever be proud to call you my sister." Before things had a chance to turn serious, he added, "So if you ever need any help with this stubborn pain-in-the-ass man with whom you've chosen to spend your life, you just let any of us know." He gestured to the other guys in the room.

"Count me in for that, too," Jeremy said with a big

smile. Everyone laughed, and damn, it felt good seeing their friends at such ease.

"So let's raise a glass to the couple who brought us all together. May love, peace, and happiness be your constant companions. To Nick and Becca." Shane raised his glass higher.

"To Nick and Becca," everyone called.

Grinning up at Nick, Becca clicked her plastic flute against his. "I love you," she said.

"Right back atcha, Sunshine," he said, his heart feeling two sizes too big for his chest. They drank.

"Is it time to eat the cake yet?" Marz said to more laughter as he leaned against the breakfast bar. Which was when Nick noticed a big cake with a figurine standing atop it next to Marz's elbow.

"Leave it to Marz to demand food," Beckett said with a smirk. Seeing Beckett relaxed and cutting it up was another big change, because for almost as long as they'd known one another, Beckett had been reserved and quiet, not one to shoot the shit or joke around. Before all this, only Marz had seemed to get behind the big guy's walls. Nick now knew that Kat had had a lot to do with how the man had changed, as much as their relationship had thrown Nick at first.

"Well, he did help me make it," Emilie said, planting a kiss on Marz's cheek. "It was all I could do to keep him from eating all the icing."

"Aw, you made this?" Becca said, stepping up to the counter. The square cake was two layers tall and read, *To Nick and Becca, The Best Is Yet To Come!* Next to the words stood a porcelain figurine of a man in fatigues embracing a blond-haired woman in a wedding dress.

And *that* was officially the first time Nick imagined seeing Becca in her wedding gown—about to get married to him. And hell if the thought of that didn't slay him.

"This is amazing, Emilie," Becca said as the women hugged.

"It really is. Thank you," Nick said, hugging Emilie next. After losing her brother—who'd been the team's enemy—her devotion to everyone in that room was truly amazing. Nick held out his hand to Marz next. "And thank you for not eating the cake before we had a chance to see it." Marz's appetite was pretty damn legendary.

Wearing his trademark grin, Marz nodded. "Dude, it was a close call." Marz could always be counted on to lighten a moment and make them laugh. Despite the fact that he'd borne the most serious injury from their ambush, he never let his amputation hold him back or get him down. Nick fucking admired that, he really did.

For a moment, surrounded by everyone he loved, Nick let himself bask in this moment of such fucking perfect contentment.

The best is yet to come.

Now that all the bullshit was behind them, Nick absolutely believed it. The future was theirs, and nothing could keep him from his happily ever after with Becca now.

"Well, what are we waiting for?" Nick asked. "Let's eat some damn cake."

Chapter Five

"I'M REALLY EXCITED to do this today," Becca said as Nick parked the car along the curb. She'd spent all her free time after work on Tuesday and Wednesday searching local venues, dress shops, caterers, florists, and other things related to planning a wedding. She already had her two days off booked with appointments, just so she could get an idea of what she'd want at her wedding.

Her wedding! Part of Becca could hardly believe it. She and Nick were getting married. She thought back to the stubborn, standoffish man she'd met that first day at Hard Ink all those months ago, and could only marvel at how far they'd come.

"Me too," Nick said. "Besides, whatever makes you happy makes me happy, you know that."

She gave him a look. "Smart man."

He grinned. "Come on. Let's go check it out."

They stepped out onto Front Street, a little cobblestone-paved gem right in the middle of downtown Baltimore. At one end of the block stood the towering 1840s Carrollton Inn and at the other, the historic Carroll Mansion, onetime home to Charles Carroll, Maryland's longest living signer of the Declaration of Independence. A brick-paved courtyard surrounded by lush gardens joined the two.

They'd barely stepped through the wrought-iron gatehouse entrance onto the property before Becca was head over heels in love—with the historic ambiance, the beautiful architecture, the whole romantic setting. A thrill of excitement shot through her. A few months ago, she'd been worried about losing her only remaining family member. Now, she'd gained a huge new family, had her brother firmly back in her life, and was about to become someone's wife. It was amazing how quickly life could change. For the good and for the bad.

"Hello," a tall woman in a smart pants suit said. With her long black hair and warm brown skin, she was strikingly pretty. "I'm Sonya Mayer, the assistant manager of the inn. Welcome." Nick and Becca introduced themselves, and Sonya gave them the tour of the inn's four interior levels and rooms, as well as its outdoor spaces.

"I can't believe I've never noticed this place before. It's just gorgeous," Becca said. The rooms each had their own unique atmosphere and decor, lending elegance to the inn's charming nineteenth-century architecture. And the courtyard would be gorgeous for an outdoor wedding, something she'd always wanted.

"We have our own little enclave back here," Sonya

said. "A little oasis of calm and historical charm in the middle of the city."

Becca nodded, struggling to keep her outward cool when inside she was all *I want it I want it and I don't care how much it costs!*

Back downstairs, Sonya guided them to a table where they had a few flower and cake samples laid out. Menus, catalogs, and price lists sat on one corner of the table atop a shiny venue folder.

"Can I offer you a glass of champagne while we talk?" Sonya asked.

"I'd love that," Becca said. "Nick?"

"Sounds great," he said. When Sonya departed, he turned to her. "Okay, tell me how much you want this place."

Becca managed to hold in her enthusiasm for about five seconds. "It's so amazing. Don't you think so? It's pretty and charming and not too big and—"

Nick kissed her. "Done."

"It's pretty expensive, though," she said.

He shook his head, his pale green eyes locked on hers. "I don't care what it costs. If you want it, we're having it. I like it, too. And we deserve the best to start our new life."

"Really?" she asked. "How'd I get so lucky?"

The smile brought out his dimple. "That's my line."

"Here we go," Sonya said, settling two crystal champagne flutes down on the table. She had an iPad tucked under her arm.

"Cheers," Nick said, clinking glasses with Becca. The champagne was sweet and bubbly, absolutely delicious.

"So, have you picked a date?" Sonya asked, bringing the iPad to life in front of her.

Becca looked to Nick. "We only just got engaged," she said. "If we wanted to have the ceremony outside, I suppose we'd need to do it by the fall or wait until the spring?" Nick nodded and gave her hand a squeeze.

"Well, let me see," Sonya said, scrolling through her digital calendar. "We're actually booking a year out right now. I know all the weekend dates in the fall are completely booked. And I think the spring is, too." Becca's shoulders dropped. She shouldn't have been surprised, really, since most people had long engagements to allow them to make their plans. "If you're interested in a shorter engagement, it looks like . . ." The woman focused on the screen for a long moment. "It looks like I only have two options as of this moment. The third Saturday in December, which would preclude an outdoor ceremony. Or, oh, we had a cancellation on Saturday, August eighth. Though if you've only just gotten engaged, I imagine that's much too soon. Otherwise, our next weekend opening is next July."

Becca barely heard anything after the August date. That was three weeks from now. She looked up at Nick. "Is three weeks from now too crazy?"

The smile he gave her made her fall even more in love with him. "Only in the best possible ways, Sunshine."

Tears pricked the backs of her eyes. "I could be your wife in three weeks."

A heated masculine satisfaction slid into those pale green eyes, and Nick turned to Sonya. "We'll take August eighth."

"IT'S A GOOD thing you'd already made an appointment to look at dresses," Emilie said as the five women piled out of Shane's big truck the following day. Sara had sweet-talked him into letting them borrow it for their girls' day out.

"I know, right?" Becca said, still floating over the fact that she was getting married in three weeks. "But the inn was just too perfect to pass up, and neither of us wanted to wait a whole year to get married."

Sara elbowed her in the side. "And you're sure this isn't a shotgun wedding, right?"

Grinning, Becca shook her head. She and Nick had been answering this question ever since they'd returned from the inn yesterday after several hours of choosing food, cake, and flowers for their event. "Nope. There's no bun in this oven, I promise you." Everyone laughed. Becca walked up to the ornate carved desk and greeted the young woman standing there. "Hi, I'm Becca Merritt."

"Welcome, Becca. Please have a seat. Diana will be right out," the woman said.

The five friends sat on the overstuffed cream-colored sofas and nibbled at cookies and fancy wrapped chocolates displayed on plates covering the glass-topped end tables. Becca and Nick might be doing this fast, but it all still felt so special to her. She was glad they weren't waiting.

A woman with short strawberry-blond hair wearing a pretty teal wrap dress approached their group. Diana made quick introductions, then took them to a sitting room where Becca could show off the gowns she tried on. "Do you have a date in mind?" Diana asked.

"I do, and it's really short notice. August eighth,"

Becca said, not missing the woman's gaze flicker down to her belly and back. Becca almost laughed. "We fell in love with a venue that had a last-minute cancellation, so we went for it."

"Well, we can make this work, Becca. We've got quite a few gowns available in our annual sample sale, so let's see if we can't find something you love. This way, please." She led them into a long rectangular room filled with racks of gowns. "Do you have any preferences for color, silhouette, length?"

"I want to wear a gown that you couldn't wear any other time," Becca said. "Something romantic and full. Maybe sleeveless. And I think I prefer white to ivory."

"Let's start with ball gowns and A-lines, then," Diana said, already pulling a few things off the racks. "Ladies, feel free to pull anything fun that you see."

Becca searched through the gowns, pulling a couple of things that caught her eye. Before long, she was in the dressing room neck deep in satin and lace and tulle. Too much tulle in the case of the first dress, which she obligingly showed to her friends even though she knew it wasn't the one. "What do you think?" she asked as she spun on the dais in front of them.

Kat made a face. "I think it's too young for you."

Sara nodded. "Too froufrou."

Becca laughed. "I agree." She tried on another, this one in a mermaid cut that wasn't at all her style. "Who picked this one?" she asked, laughing.

"What? I thought it was cool," Sara's younger sister, Jenna, said. They both had matching red hair.

"Sadly, I don't have the hips to pull this off. Or the boobs. Or whatever else you need to make this work." Becca rolled her eyes as the women nodded and laughed. The third one was closer—a sleeveless ball-gown style with lots of lace and beading. "This is gorgeous," Becca said. "But it's so heavy I don't know how I'd dance in it."

"I don't know, Becca," Emilie said, tucking her brown hair behind her ears. "That one might be worth suffering for."

It took five more dresses before Becca fell in love. The white ball gown had a sleeveless sweetheart neckline and gorgeous beading at the waist, while the skirt fell in soft layers of satin, full but not poofy. It was two sizes too big and was missing a few buttons down the back, but Diana assured her it could be taken in and repaired in plenty of time. Staring in the mirror, Becca suddenly felt overwhelmed.

Kat was the first one to notice. She crossed from the sofa to stand beside Becca. "You okay?"

Afraid that trying to speak might hasten the threatening tears, Becca just nodded.

"This is the one, isn't it?" Kat met Becca's gaze in the mirror. Despite her petite stature, Kat looked so much like her brothers, with her chocolate brown hair and green eyes—and even a few shared facial expressions— that Becca immediately felt at ease. And she realized there was something she needed to ask Katherine.

"Yeah," Becca managed. "I don't need to look anymore." She turned to face Kat. "Will you be my maid of honor?" They might not have known each other very long, but in the few months since they'd met, they'd bonded hard and fast, not only over their love for the Rixey men but also because of the way Kat had taken care of Becca during the team's investigation.

Kat's eyes went wide. "You want me?"

"We're going to be sisters, right? I absolutely want you. If you'll do it," Becca said.

Kat hugged her. "I'd love to stand up for you and Nick. I'm so happy for both of you."

"Okay, now. Don't make me cry. I'm having a hard enough time with that as it is," Becca said. Everyone laughed. Becca gave herself one last look in the mirror. "Yeah, this is the one." She turned to see the back of it, all clean, soft lines of satin. On her shoulder, the healing tattoo peeked out through her hair. The design was as beautiful as the words were appropriate, so she had no qualms about the ink showing. She was proud of the gift Nick had given her.

"Well, then," Diana said. "Let's get the tailor to take a look at you, and then we'll get the ladies started on bridesmaid dresses. Any idea what color you'd like?"

"Yes," Becca said. "Kat, can you grab the picture from my purse?" Kat handed Diana the picture of the bridesmaids' bouquets Becca had chosen. "I figured it might be hard to get one bridesmaid dress that works for everyone in the short time we have," Becca continued. "So as long as the gown is a shade of purple that matches these flowers, I don't care what style or length it is. Whatever you guys like."

Diana studied the picture, which showed a bouquet

with mauve roses, purple hydrangeas, dark purple irises, berry-colored orchids, burgundy dahlias, and light purple mini carnations. "Oh, yes, we can make this work. I'll grab the tailor for you and show the girls where to look."

In the time it took for Becca to get fitted, everyone found things to try on. And it didn't take long until all four friends decided on dresses that suited their taste and matched Becca's color scheme. Kat chose a sleek, sleeveless dark-purple gown that looked gorgeous with her long brown hair. Emilie picked a mauve V-neck gown with a satin belt at the waist. Sara chose a satin berry-colored sheath with cap sleeves and a sweetheart neckline, while Jenna went with a flirty lavender gown with a drop waist and a fuller skirt that accentuated her curves beautifully.

"You all look stunning," Becca said when they stood before her. "The guys aren't going to know what to do with themselves."

"Shane's never seen me in a dress like this before," Sara said, staring at herself in the mirror. "In fact, I don't think I've ever owned a dress like this before."

Jenna grasped her sister's hand. Despite being the youngest of the five of them, the Dean sisters had been through hell the past few years, especially Sara, who'd borne the burden of repaying her criminal father's debts after he'd died, sometimes in ways too horrible to imagine. "Well, it won't be the last one," Jenna said, smiling. "But, yeah, it's gonna be fun seeing their reactions."

"I think we're all pretty guaranteed to get laid at Becca's wedding," Kat said with a mischievous grin.

They all burst into laughter. "When do you *not* get laid, Kat?" Emilie asked with an arched eyebrow.

"Aw, don't even talk to me, Miss Garza, because you and Marz are loud as hell. Not that I mind, because, *dude*, does he have a mouth on him," Kat said with a big grin.

"Oh, my God," Sara said, her cheeks turning bright pink but her smile saying she was enjoying the teasing.

"He really does." Grinning, Emilie shrugged. "The hazards of sharing an unfinished apartment. Can't be helped." Kat and Beckett had been staying in the room Nick and Jeremy reserved for her in their apartment until one particularly loud session of lovemaking had apparently caught Jer's ear. His teasing had been relentless. Finally, Kat and Beckett relocated to an empty room upstairs. As much as they all enjoyed each other's company, everyone was going to be thrilled when the new building was done, that was for sure.

Becca could only laugh as the good-natured ribbing went on. "Well, I know I'm getting laid. The rest of you are on your own." By the time they'd all been fitted and had paid for their gowns, Becca was pretty sure they were on the verge of getting thrown out of the store.

They spilled out onto the street, laughing and hungry for lunch. Becca fell behind while she fished for her cell phone in her purse and paused to shoot off a quick text to Nick.

All done dress shopping! I'm gonna knock your socks off! ;)

Nick responded immediately. *Sunshine, you already do.* Grinning, she glanced down the block—and nearly gasped out loud. Tyrell Woodson stood at the corner, glaring at her.

"Hey, Becca, come on," Kat called. Becca blinked and the man was gone. Vanished. A figment of her imagination. Not that her body seemed to know the difference. Heart racing, she caught up with the group as they made their way to an Italian place they'd agreed on earlier. "You okay?" Kat asked.

"Yeah. Great." Her voice sounded flat to her own ears. She glanced back over her shoulder. Woodson wasn't there. Of course. She let out a long breath. She'd gotten through the whole workweek without another incident like the one she'd had with Ben at the end of her first shift back. Clearly, her subconscious wasn't done worrying about Woodson, though, however unnecessary—and unfounded—that worrying was.

Why was she freaking out about what'd happened to her now? For months, she'd been fine, just an occasional nightmare of being grabbed, being dragged away, being lost and never found. Then again, for most of that time she'd been shut up at Hard Ink with Nick.

They arrived at the restaurant, and Kat paused before she followed the others inside. "Are you sure you're okay?" she asked. "Because you know my brother will kill me if anything happens to you on my watch." Kat arched an eyebrow. Though Becca knew she was joking, there'd been a time not too long before when Kat had in fact been Becca's bodyguard, during a meeting with the man who'd turned out to be responsible for the death of Becca's dad. Nick had gotten angry at both of them when they'd had to deviate from the original plan to get Becca home safely.

"You just survived heart surgery, Kat," Becca said. Kat had gotten shot at the same funeral where Jeremy had been hurt. Watching Nick deal with both of his siblings fighting for their lives was one of the hardest things Becca had ever done. But they'd both pulled through. And now they all deserved a celebration. "Nick is so grateful you're okay that I'm pretty sure you'll be able to get away with absolutely anything for the rest of your life," Becca said with a smile. "And I'm fine, I promise."

"Good," Kat said, giving her a last look. "Then let's eat, because I'm starving."

Chapter Six

IT HAPPENED AGAIN the next week. More than once. Most recently, it occurred on her way back to the hospital after grabbing something for lunch. Becca saw Woodson lurking in a doorway farther down the street, but when she looked again, no one was there.

That night, as she and Nick lay in bed, Becca gave voice to the question whose answer she thought might best give her some peace of mind. "Do you know what happened to Tyrell Woodson after you interrogated him?"

Nick shifted to look at her, concern filling his pale green eyes. "Why?"

"I just wondered," she said, feeling a little bad for not sharing what she'd been experiencing. She didn't want to worry him, though, especially when they had so much going on—the construction, setting up his and the team's new business, her work at the ER, planning the wedding. During their off hours this week, they'd managed to send out invitations, find an officiant, hire a DJ, and apply for their marriage license. Luckily, all the guys already had their dress blues from when the Army had held a memorial service for the fallen members of their A-team a few weeks before.

Eyes narrowed, Nick studied her. "You know we sent the harbor police out to that island where we dropped him, but he was gone when they got there. So once Detective Vance joined our investigation, I had him search for Woodson. Just to be on the safe side."

Gone? Becca pushed up onto an elbow. Vance's inquiry was news to her. "So what did he find?"

Nick tucked her hair behind her ear. "Woodson's not in custody anywhere, but he's not here. Vance tracked him to South Carolina using credit card transactions. Apparently he has family down there. Looks like he left town right after everything went down. Marz took that video of him spilling all kinds of secrets. No doubt he wanted to get clear of the city in case we turned it over to Church like we threatened."

Relief flooded through Becca so fast that she sagged back down to her pillow. He wasn't in Baltimore. Hell, he wasn't in Maryland. So it really was her imagination at work. "Oh. That's good."

Leaning over her, Nick cupped Becca's face in his hand. "Shit, Becca. I'm sorry. Have you been worrying about this? I should've said something, but—"

"No, not worried, exactly. I guess I just needed to know. For closure." And it was true. Maybe she could stop seeing ghosts around every corner now.

Nick nodded. "Why don't I have Vance run another trace on him? Make sure he's still out of the picture? I can't imagine why he'd come back with how volatile Baltimore's gang scene is right now. Since the Church Gang imploded, Louis Jackson told us that the word on the street for former Churchmen is leave or die. It's been open season on them as other gangs fight to consolidate power and take over the heroin trade."

Becca nodded, Nick's words strengthening the bulwarks against her fear. "Yeah, that makes sense. But have Vance run the check. It can't hurt, right?"

"Absolutely. You know I'd do anything to keep you safe, Becca." He nailed her with a stare full of such fierce love that it stole her breath.

"Of course. And so would I," she said.

It only took the weekend before Vance had news. He called Monday night after Becca's shift while everyone was hanging out watching movies in Nick and Jeremy's living room.

"Vance," Nick said as he answered his cell and got up from the couch. "How are you?"

"Want me to pause it?" Jeremy asked, sitting in the corner of the other couch next to Charlie, Eileen attempting to fit her growing body on his lap.

Nick waved him off and headed back down the hall toward his office. Becca followed. "And what did you find?" Nick asked as he settled into the chair at his desk. As Becca looked at him sitting there, memories came rushing back. One of her first nights here. Giving Nick a massage after his back had been hurt when he and Beckett had gotten into a fistfight. How he'd kissed her. "Well, that's good news then."

The words pulled Becca from her thought. Good news had to mean Woodson was still far away, right?

"Okay, sounds like a plan. Thanks, man," Nick said.

"What did he say?" she asked when Nick hung up.

He tossed his cell to the desk and reached out for her, pulling her down to straddle his lap. "As recently as last Wednesday, Woodson got a speeding ticket in South Carolina. Vance is still working on recent credit card transactions. But that's pretty good evidence that he's stayed put." Nick stroked his fingers through Becca's hair. "Vance is going to put out a be-on-the-lookout for Woodson's car with local PD, on the off chance he returns to the area."

Becca nodded. "That all sounds good. Thank you for having him do that."

"A little extra peace of mind never hurts," he said. Hand slipping behind her neck, he gently pulled her down until their lips met. The kiss was slow and soft and exploring, full of the heat that always flared quickly to life between them. "You're gonna be my wife in less than two weeks," he whispered around the edge of the kiss.

The words made her smile. "I am." The kiss deepened. "Yours to do with whatever you want."

Nick's gaze flashed hot. "My thoughts exactly." He urged her to stand up, then he crossed to the door and closed it. When he turned to her, the expression on his face was predatory, so damn sexy she was immediately wet with anticipation. Without a word, he stood in front of her, unbuttoned and pushed down her jeans and panties, and sank to his knees in front of her. "Right now what I want is for you to come all over my tongue."

Becca clutched onto the desk behind her as Nick planted his mouth between her legs, his tongue immediately plunging into her folds and finding her clit. Together they worked her jeans the rest of the way off, then Nick pushed her stance wider and settled his big body in tight between her legs.

He was relentless, his fingers holding her open, his tongue alternating between lapping at her and hard, fast flicks, his mouth sucking.

"Oh, God, Nick," she rasped, her hand falling on his hair and clutching at it. He growled against her, not letting up for a second, and she thrust her hips forward, yearning and seeking and craving even more. She tugged his hair, pulling him in tighter, unable to restrain herself from demanding what she needed.

And it seemed to drive Nick harder, because he worked a thick finger inside her slickness and sucked her in a fast rhythm that had her panting and thrusting and straining. The orgasm hit her like a shock wave, not there one moment and then throwing her head over heels the next. She got light-headed and her knees went soft, forcing her to sag back against the desk.

"Holy shit," she rasped.

Nick eased his hand free of her and looked up, his gaze so full of smug satisfaction that it made her shake her head as she smiled. And then, eyes on hers, he sucked the wetness off his finger and licked his lips. "You taste fucking delicious, Sunshine."

Becca's heart did a little flip as she offered him a hand and he rose. "You know," she said, "if I hadn't already agreed to marry you, I would say yes just based on how good you are at that."

Nick threw his head back and laughed, the kind of free, joyful laughter she'd only heard from him a handful of times. His smile was freaking gorgeous, his dimple a mile deep, and his face so ruggedly beautiful that it made her whole chest ache with how much she loved him. "Good to know," he managed.

Grinning, she wrapped her arms around his neck. "Seriously. A man who can make the best Sloppy Joes on earth, helps total strangers, sings bad eighties anthems, loves his family fiercely, can kill in fifty-two ways if he has to, is smoking hot, *and* eats pussy like he's starved for it is a keeper." She tried to keep a straight face, but laughter was already bubbling up inside her.

"I . . . am really freaking aroused now. Keep talking," he said, his eyebrow arched, that smug smile returning.

She reached for his jeans and tugged the button open. "About what? Should I talk about how much I love your cock? How amazing it feels inside me?"

Nick licked his lips, a kind of amused disbelief filling his gaze. "Yes, definitely talk about that. Like, a lot."

Grinning, Becca bit her lip and pushed off the desk. Walking backward, she hooked her fingers in the waistband of his jeans and pulled him along with her toward the bedroom. With her other hand, she grasped his hard length, squeezing just enough to wring a grunt out of him. "Come put this inside me, Nick, and I'll say absolutely anything you want."

NICK FELT LIKE he hadn't seen Becca in forever, despite the fact that they'd woken up together this morning. But that had been fifteen hours ago—before he'd spent all day working with the guys to install the carpet in their new offices. As much as possible, they were trying to do the work on the business suite to allow the contractor to stay focused on the much bigger project of the building. Given Jeremy's ability to figure out pretty much any home improvement project, Beckett's electrical know-how, and Marz and Charlie's expertise with all the wiring and secure computer hookups they needed done, they were in pretty good shape.

In the meantime, all of them had been working their contacts to get word out about the new security consulting services they'd be offering. Beckett, Marz, and Shane had already been working in various aspects of the field and had ready clients to reach out to. Having worked for years as a computer security consultant hacking into corporations' systems to find their weaknesses, Charlie turned out to be an amazing asset in making new contacts. All of which was keeping them on track for a targeted post–Labor Day opening date, which would give Nick and Becca two weeks for their honeymoon in Italy and another two for Nick to be back and helping with all the last-minute prep.

Nick's and Beckett's cell phones dinged an incoming message at about the same time, and both of them paused where they knelt on the floor to check their phones. Since Becca and Kat had gone shopping together after Becca's half-day shift, Nick didn't have to guess at who it was.

On the way home. Be there in about twenty! xo

"Aw, look at you two," Shane said, his tone full of sarcasm. "Stop chitchatting with the ladies and let's get this shit finished."

"You are as pussy-whipped as any of us, McCallan, so shut the fuck up," Beckett said as he shoved his phone in his back pocket. Ah, it was so nice that they were all getting along so good again. Just like old times. In all the best ways.

From the next room where Marz and Charlie were working on some wiring, Charlie called, "For the record, I am not as pussy-whipped as the rest of you."

Silence rang out for a moment, and then they all lost their shit. Just flat-out, tear-inducing laughter that had every one of them clutching their guts. Charlie fucking Merritt was coming out of his shell, that was for goddamn sure.

Wiping the tears from his eyes, Nick managed to get to two feet and make it to the doorway, where he found Marz red in the face with hilarity and Jeremy pressing a big kiss to his boyfriend's mouth. The affection his brother and soon-to-be brother-in-law bore for each other made Nick happy, it really did. Because Nick had never seen Jeremy settle down like this before—with a man or a woman, and he'd dated both. And no matter how much

Nick admired so many other things about Becca and Charlie's father—the team's former commander—Nick would never understand the homophobic bullshit Frank Merritt had apparently rained down on Charlie from the moment he'd come out. So Charlie deserved this chance to be happy and loved and accepted. By all of them. And, amazingly, they all fit together like clockwork—even Jeremy and Charlie, who hadn't been part of their team.

They were now.

Beckett joined Nick in the doorway, his bright blue eyes gleaming. "Tou-fucking-che, Charlie."

Because he had his hair pulled back in some sort of a bun thing, the red covering Charlie's face was crystal clear, but the guy was smiling as Marz slapped him on the knee.

Everyone got back to work, shooting the shit as they finished up the last of the carpeting.

From where he knelt in the corner, Easy ran his dark hand over his short-trimmed hair and looked around the nearly finished space. "This is all really coming together."

"Yes, it is," Nick said. Right now, it was all plain white walls and industrial gray carpeting, but they'd come a helluva long way from the cement floor, exposed ceilings, and cinder-block walls that had stood there just a few weeks before. "Thanks to the hard work you all have been putting in."

"I'm glad to do it," Easy said. "It's good to be busy. And it's really fucking good to feel like I'm part of some-thing again."

Nick, Easy, Beckett, and Shane all traded looks and

nodded. Every one of them felt the same way after the ambush, the other-than-honorable discharge, having their reputations tarnished, and being scattered to the four winds once they'd returned stateside.

"Amen, brother," Shane said, clapping Easy on the shoulder.

When the other three men cleared out, Nick went into the next room to see how the wiring job was coming. "Almost done?" he asked Marz.

"Yeah, hoss. Maybe just another half hour," Marz said. Charlie nodded.

"Anything I can do to help?" Nick asked.

"Nope, we're good. If you see Em, just let her know I'll be up in a bit." Kneeling in front of some cables sticking out of the wall, Marz kneaded absentmindedly at his thigh.

Nick frowned. "You okay?" Sometimes you could almost forget about Marz's amputation because the guy never let it slow him down, even when he should.

"Hmm?" Marz looked up from the complicated jack he was working on. "Oh, yeah. No worries. Damn leg just gets cranky if I spend much time on the floor."

"I told you I'd do that." Charlie paused what he'd been coding on his laptop to look at Marz.

"I'm fine. And this is the last one anyway. Go see your bride-to-be." Marz looked up at Nick with a grin.

Nick nodded. "All right. Later." He stepped through the back door out into the warm July night and nearly walked into Beckett. "Sorry. What's the matter?" Nick asked, noticing the serious expression Beckett wore.

Beckett shook his head. "I just made Becca cry."

Frowning, Nick glanced around the otherwise empty parking lot. Kat's car was there, so they were back. "What?" he asked, heading toward the door to the main part of the Hard Ink building.

Beckett fell into step beside him. "I came up behind her and Kat out here, and when Becca noticed me, she freaked out. Nearly jumped out of her skin. At first she tried to play it off, but then she got upset and ran inside."

Nick punched the code into the keypad, and they stepped into the concrete-and-metal stairwell that led to Hard Ink on the first floor and their apartments and the gym on the upper floors. "Don't worry about it. I'm sure she's fine."

Beckett gave him a doubtful look but nodded. "Let me know if there's anything I can do."

Clapping him on the arm, Nick shook his head. "I'll take care of her." They parted ways as Nick let himself into his apartment and Beckett made his way upstairs. The big open kitchen and living room were empty. "Becca?" he called, an urgent need to see her and make sure she was okay flowing through him.

No answer. He went straight for their rooms at the back of the apartment.

"You need to tell him," someone said. Kat.

"I agree," came another voice. Emilie?

Nick rounded the corner into his office to see Becca sitting on his sofa, her face wet with tears. Kat and Emilie sat on either side of her. Nick's gut dropped to the floor. "Tell me what?"

Chapter Seven

NICK NAILED BECCA with a stare. As he watched, she made a valiant effort to button up just how upset she was, and that made him worry even more. He knelt down in front of her, his hands on her knees. "What's going on?"

She shook her head, and his heart fucking broke as he saw her struggle to find her voice and hold back the tears.

Kat grasped something from Becca's lap and held it out to him. "Someone left this in front of Becca's locker at work today."

Frowning, Nick accepted the small, floppy, black-and-brown stuffed animal into his hand. He guessed it was supposed to be a German shepherd, and the damn thing was missing a leg. It looked like someone had cut the back leg off and stapled the opening closed. What the hell?

"Look at the neck, Nick," Kat said, her voice serious.

He flipped it around, and that was when he noticed that the animal was so floppy because the head was connected to the body only by a thin strip of material along the back. He might not have thought much about that if someone hadn't gone to the trouble of spray painting the torn opening red. As if the neck had been slit. "Sonofabitch," he said, hot prickles running down his back. "Talk to me, Sunshine."

She heaved a deep breath. "I found it at the end of my shift," she said. "I went to get my stuff, and this was sitting upright on the floor in front of my locker. I thought someone had left me a present until . . ."

"This is fucking twisted," Kat bit out.

The words echoed Nick's own thoughts. Twisted and threatening. The removed leg was clearly meant to communicate that the person knew Becca's dog had only three legs, which made the threat personal and specific. "Did you talk to security about this?" he asked, making sure to keep his voice even.

Becca shook her head. "I was so freaked out, I just wanted to get out of there."

"I didn't know about this until just now, or I would've brought us home earlier," Kat said.

"I'm sorry," Becca said, turning to Nick's sister. "I just wanted to forget about it for a few hours."

"I know," Kat said. "You don't have to apologize, but I'm worried about this."

Nick nodded. "Can you think of anyone at the hospital who would do this? Who would have a problem with you?"

"I know some people are upset that I've asked for time off for the wedding and our honeymoon after being on leave for two months." Becca scrubbed her face with her hands. "I overheard some women talking at the nurse's station yesterday. But I can't imagine anyone doing something this cruel. And twisted. Kat's right."

"I don't like it, Becca," Nick said, his hackles all up. "I don't like it at all. I'd like to go with you tomorrow to talk to hospital security. They need to know."

She gave a quick nod. "Okay."

"Is this why you freaked out when Beckett came up behind you out back?" he asked.

Becca sagged back against the couch. "Partly."

Nick frowned, his instincts flaring. "What's the other part?"

The quick look Becca exchanged with Emilie had Nick's gut twisting with worry, especially when Em gave her a small nod. "I know it's ridiculous," Becca said in a small voice, "but I keep thinking I'm seeing Woodson."

The words hung there for a moment and rushed ice through Nick's veins.

Emilie got up and gestured for Nick to sit. He slid onto the couch next to Becca. He'd barely put his arm around her shoulders when she buried her face against his chest, her arm clutching his neck. Her shoulders shook with restrained tears. "Aw, Becca," he said, his heart absolutely aching. How had he not seen this?

"I'm sorry," she rasped.

He locked eyes with Kat, whose expression was every bit as concerned and upset as he felt. "You don't have anything to apologize for. You hear me?"

A quick nod against his chest.

Guilt flooded into his gut. Why hadn't he ever considered that the attempted abductions might have traumatized Becca? She'd been so strong through it all that he'd just assumed she was fine. No wonder she'd asked him what had happened to Woodson. Yet, once again, he hadn't probed deep enough. "Shit, I'm the one who should be apologizing." He stroked her hair.

"No," she said, shaking her head as she pulled away. Her face was red and wet and her eyes were puffy, but she was still the most beautiful thing he'd ever seen. "How could you have known? It just felt so ridiculous that I didn't want to say anything."

"Tell me what's been going on," he said, cupping her cheek in his palm and swiping at her tears with his thumb.

She gave a shy little shrug. "I keep thinking I see him. One minute he's there, and the next he's not. At random times. Around the hospital. On the street. Tonight at the mall I kept feeling like someone was watching me, but of course no one was there. Just like no one's ever there. I was just freaked out about the stuffed animal. After all that, Beckett just scared me and everything kinda crashed in on me." The words spilled out of her in a rush.

"It's not ridiculous, Becca," Emilie said. "It's PTSD." Before all this, Emilie had worked as a clinical psychologist at a local university. Given the shit all of them had been through, she'd been an incredible resource for the whole team these past months.

"But I was fine," Becca said, looking from Nick to Emilie to Kat. "I was fine after it happened."

"The crisis of the investigation probably kept your brain otherwise focused. But then you went back to the scene of the abduction, and you were out on your own for the first time in months." Emilie knelt where Nick had been. "Your nervous system is finally trying to process what happened to you. The anxiety, the reliving of the event, the spontaneous memories, the paranoia. These are all normal given what you went through."

The list of symptoms lashed at Nick's soul. He hated that Becca was hurting. Was the shit that had happened in Afghanistan never going to stop raining down on them? "She's right," Nick said, taking Becca's hand. "How frequently has this been happening?"

Becca frowned, and her gaze went distant. "Maybe a half dozen times since I started back to work."

"Aw, Sunshine," Nick said. He hated that she'd been carrying this all by herself. But no more. "What can I do to help?"

"I don't know," Becca said. "I know it's not real. But I can't seem to make it stop."

"It's gonna take time," Emilie said. "I can help you with some techniques to reduce and combat anxiety. Or you might consider seeing a therapist at the hospital."

"Okay," Becca said. "I'd like to talk to you, I think."

Emilie nodded.

"Maybe you should consider taking off even earlier than you planned," Kat said. Nick could've hugged her, because his thoughts were running in the same direction. But the last thing Becca needed was for him to be an overprotective asshole right now.

"I only have four and a half more shifts," Becca said. "I'd hate to bail on everyone last minute."

"Becca," Kat said, taking her other hand. "You're always taking care of everyone else. You have to let us take care of you, too."

"I know," Becca said in a small voice. "I think if we address this stuffed animal with the hospital and I'm talking to Emilie, I'll feel better."

"That's a good start," Nick said. "But until you take off, I'm walking you in and out of the hospital at the beginning and end of your shifts. If you have wedding errands you need to do, I want to be at your side. And, hey," he said, gently turning her face toward him. "Please talk to me. I can't be there for you if you don't let me know what you need."

Nodding, Becca gave him a look that nearly broke his fucking heart. "I just didn't want to worry you."

He lifted her left hand to his mouth and kissed her ring, then he pressed her hand to his heart. "Taking care of you is my job, Sunshine. For the rest of my life. In good times and in bad, remember?"

Glassiness filled her eyes. "Yeah."

Kat rose, and Emilie followed suit. "We'll give you guys some time alone," Kat said. She leaned over and pressed a kiss against the top of Becca's head. "I had fun shopping with you, sis."

It was the first smile he'd seen from Becca since he'd walked into the room. "I had fun with you, too, Kat," Becca said. "You're going to be the best sister ever."

"Hey, I already am," Kat said with a grin. She and Emilie left.

"Can we get ready for bed?" Becca asked in a small voice. "I'd really like to just lay down with you."

"Of course," Nick said, helping her up. They got changed without talking much, then he climbed into bed and held his arm open to her. Becca crawled in alongside his body and fitted herself tight against his side, like she always did. She fit so fucking perfectly against him. Nick stroked his fingers through her hair. "I don't want you to ever feel like you can't talk to me. About anything."

"I know. I do feel like I can," Becca said, shifting to meet his gaze. Her eyes were so blue. "I should've said something sooner. I'm sorry."

"I get it," Nick said. "I do. But the best thing about having a team is you get help carrying the load. You and me. We're a team now."

Becca smiled. "Always and forever."

"That's fucking right."

"I won't forget again," she said.

"You didn't forget, Sunshine. You're still just getting used to the idea. Me too." He hugged her in against him. "It's hard to lean on someone else when you've been so used to walking on your own."

She nodded. "I love you, Nick."

"I love you, too. There's nothing to worry about. I promise you," he said. And Nick was going to do whatever it took to make that the truth.

WHILE BECCA WAS in the shower the next morning, Nick let the guys know what was going on. Standing around the island in the kitchen, he said, "Becca is dealing with some PTSD from the abduction attempts. Probably triggered by returning to work, the scene of the first attack. And she keeps thinking she's seeing Woodson."

"Damn," Beckett said. "We all saw how roughly he treated her when he tried to grab her the second time. It's no wonder she's struggling."

Nick nodded, the memory souring the coffee in his gut. "Vance has given me some circumstantial evidence that places Woodson in South Carolina, where he's been since we interrogated him, but just keep your eyes open. Be on the lookout. I'm going to do a little more digging there to make sure Becca's not discounting something that's really there."

"Can't be too careful," Beckett said.

"No, not with Becca. That's for damn sure."

"This place is about as secure as we can make it," Marz said. "So we're good here. And the cameras from around the neighborhood are still up and running, so if you have Woodson's vehicle specs, I can keep an eye out. Make sure nothing's hanging around that shouldn't be."

"Do that," Nick said. "Thanks. I'm going to talk to hospital security this morning about this damn thing." He pointed to the stuffed animal, sitting in a plastic bag on the counter.

"Sick fuck," Shane said, glaring at it. "You should let Vance know about this, too."

"I will. I've got a whole to-do list on this today. I'm going to talk to Vance after I leave the hospital, and then I'm going to drop by the inn and work with them to beef up the event security they already provide. I don't want Becca thinking about anything besides having a good time on our wedding day."

Nods all around.

"What am I missing? Can you think of anything else?" Nick asked.

"Would it make her feel any better to carry a weapon?" Shane asked, his gaze serious.

"Good question. I'll talk to her about it. She doesn't have a concealed carry permit, though, and even though some of us flouted that law the past couple of months, I don't know if she'd be comfortable doing so." Though Nick and Beckett had had Maryland permits, the other guys were from out of state and hadn't. Carrying illegally was just one of the ways they'd had to work outside the law to clear their names. Now that they were opening a security firm of their own, all the guys were in compliance. Their business was going to have to be run completely by the book.

"Maybe you should get in contact with Chen," Beckett said. "If Vance can't track Woodson down, Chen sure as hell should be able to. He fucking owes us anyway."

Nick nodded. "True. I'll do that." Chen was the CIA operative who'd first assigned Frank Merritt to the undercover corruption investigation in Afghanistan that had snowballed into the shit storm of the last year. When Nick and his team had rescued Charlie and picked up the investigation, Chen had found them and offered the vital assistance that had finally allowed the team to take down the bad guys and clear their own names. Chen wanted them to work for the CIA from time to time, which meant he was predisposed to do them favors. And Nick wasn't above asking.

"Hey," Becca said, walking into the kitchen. Wearing a set of lavender scrubs, she looked fresh faced and beautiful. His sunshine.

"Hey," Nick said, hugging her in against him. "Want a bagel before we go?"

"Sure," she said.

Nick busied himself with the task, then turned around to find Easy wrapping her in his arms. "I'm here for you, Becca," he said in a quiet voice. One by one, the men repeated the action and the words. *This* was what family looked like. It made Nick fucking proud. And, truth be told, it choked him up. Just a little.

An hour later, they were sitting across the desk from the hospital's chief security officer, a tall, wiry man with graying blond hair and a weather-beaten face. Barry Coleman had served for twenty years in the Marine Corps and worked in security for the past eight, facts that already made Nick feel a little better about leaving Becca there today.

Becca recounted when and how she'd found the stuffed animal, and Coleman asked a series of probing questions. Finally, he said, "Unfortunately, we don't have a security camera inside the staff break room. After Becca's attack, we secured and alarmed that external door, and we put cameras on all the main entrances into the ER, but I'll have one installed in there today. Just for some extra peace of mind. And I'll get my team on reviewing the personnel rosters and camera feeds from yesterday to see if we can pull together a list of people to talk to. This is harassment and intimidation, Becca, and we won't tolerate it for a second. I can promise you."

"Thank you," she said.

"In case it needs to be said, there's no chance Tyrell Woodson could get in here again. We have photographs of him posted at all the monitors. The whole security team knows what he looks like, including the BPD officers stationed in the waiting room," Coleman said.

"We have reason to believe he's out of the area anyway," Nick said. "We heard South Carolina."

Coleman nodded. "That's good to know. We'll get to the bottom of this, I promise."

Nick shook the man's hand, then he and Becca walked out through the back part of the ER. In the break room, Becca stowed her purse in her locker. "You sure you're okay being here?" Nick asked, his hands rubbing her shoulders. "No one would blame you for cutting out a few days early."

"I want to do this," Becca said. "I promise I'm okay. And I wouldn't hesitate to go to Coleman if something happened."

Nick nodded. "Okay. I'll be here at three to walk you out. Have a good day, Sunshine."

She smiled. "You, too. I can't wait to celebrate tonight."

"Me too," Nick said. Tonight all of them were having dinner together at a great local steak house before parting ways for their respective bachelor and bachelorette parties. Nick kissed her for a long moment, and he didn't want to admit how hard he found it to walk away and leave her.

But he had things he needed to do today to give them *both* some peace of mind. Vance, Chen, the inn. Nick also wanted to drive by Woodson's last known address and make sure nothing was going on down there. Anything to help Becca feel better and get past the way his life had exploded all over hers.

It was the least he could do.

Chapter Eight

THAT NIGHT AT dinner, Nick couldn't keep his hands off Becca. Despite the fantastic food, the great company of friends, and the well-deserved celebration, all he wanted was to get Becca alone somewhere so he could flip up the flirty skirt on the stunning little yellow dress she'd worn and get inside her any and every way he could.

Part of it was the top-shelf liquor flowing all around the table, and part of it was the relief Nick felt after all his efforts today had panned out in one way or another. Vance had found a parking ticket on Woodson's car from two days ago in South Carolina, and Chen had agreed to put his considerable resources into not only pinpointing the guy's location but also getting him off the street once and for all. The inn had agreed to additional security, and the head of the security company they used had even made the time to meet with Nick. The guy and his team seemed competent, smart, and savvy, so there was another thing on their side. And Woodson's last known address had not only been quiet as a grave but dust-covered to boot. No one had been there any time recently.

That still left the mystery of the stuffed animal, of course, but Coleman was on it, and Becca's day at work had been incident-free. They'd get to the bottom of that yet.

Becca had been visibly relieved when Nick had filled her in on his day. Now, she seemed so relaxed and happy that it made his fucking heart ache.

Sitting at the dinner table surrounded by their friends, Nick squeezed her thigh. She turned to him wearing a huge smile, a champagne glass in her hand. "Are you feeling frisky, Mr. Rixey?" she asked.

Nick leaned in close. "No, I'm fucking horny. I want to mess up your lipstick and tear off your panties and make my fingers and cock smell like you." He leaned back again, his face carefully neutral.

Her eyes were wide—and full of heat. "Holy shit. How am I supposed to be apart from you the rest of the night after that?"

"Welcome to my world, Sunshine." He threw back a gulp of whiskey.

"Come here. I want to taste that off your tongue," she said.

"Jesus," he gritted out, but it wasn't like he was turning down a kiss. She leaned in, giving him a great view of her cleavage down the front of her sequined strapless dress, and grasped his face in her hand. Her lips were warm, soft, and tasted like champagne and the chocolate mousse cake they'd shared for dessert. Fucking delicious.

Her tongue slipped around his, and she pressed herself closer.

"Someone pull those two apart," one of the guys yelled.

Nick grinned even as they continued to kiss. He wasn't voluntarily giving up Becca's mouth, that was for goddamned sure.

"All right," Kat said from the other side of Nick. "We better get the rest of the night underway before we lose the bride and groom." Laughter all around as everyone got up from the table.

"Do you think they'd notice if we snuck away?" Becca asked, her face absolutely glowing.

Beckett grabbed Nick by the shoulders. "Get up, Rix. The tables are waiting for us."

"Apparently," Nick said. "You go have a good time, Sunshine. But you be ready for me later." He arched a brow.

"Oh, I will," Becca said, her tongue licking at her bottom lip.

Shit, he had it bad for her. And he fucking loved it. This woman was going to be his *wife*. How fantastically lucky was he? A man who just months ago would've said he didn't believe in luck, unless it was of the bad kind.

Outside, they found two massive stretch Hummer limousines waiting for them. Beckett had arranged their transportation for the evening through one of the companies he had experience working with—the cars were bulletproof and the drivers were prior military and armed. Nick appreciated the hell out of the gesture.

As the men headed for one vehicle and the women for the other, Nick pulled Becca into his arms. "Have fun, Sunshine. I love you."

"Love you, too, Nick." This kiss was softer, sweeter. Which was good, since all their friends started giving them shit.

"Yeah, yeah," Nick said, flipping the guys the finger. "Before you go, I have something for you," he murmured, then slipped a little wrapped box into Becca's hand. "Wear this and think of me."

"What is it?" she asked.

"I'm not telling," he said. Finding this present had been the other good thing he'd accomplished while she'd been at work.

With a little wave and a big grin, Becca turned to catch up with the women, her skirt twirling out and showing a dangerous amount of thigh. God, she looked gorgeous.

When she was safely tucked inside the Hummer and it pulled away from the curb, Nick got into his own limo and Shane pushed a fresh glass of whiskey into his hand. "Gentlemen, start your livers," Shane called out, loosening his tie and raising a glass of his own.

A round of laughter as everyone drank and the limo started moving. Colored lights ran around the tops of the leather seats, and a fully stocked bar filled one whole side.

Marz sat forward in his seat, a mischievous grin on his face. "If the ocean was vodka and I was a duck, I'd swim to the bottom and drink it all up. But the ocean's not vodka and I'm not a duck, so pass me the bottle and—"

"Let's get fucked up!" they all finished.

"Fuckin' A," Marz said with a laugh.

Beckett rolled up the sleeves of his dress shirt and held up his glass. With a sly grin, he said, "I'll keep mine short and sweet. May all your ups and downs be between the sheets."

"Hear fucking hear," Nick said, taking a drink and laughing at the blush filling Charlie's cheeks. He and Jer were in for a rude awakening—Nick's teammates were fucking fish, and it'd been a damn long time since they'd had a night like this to just cut loose. Hell, it'd been way more than a year since they'd last done it together.

"All right," Easy said, holding up his glass. "I'll play."

"Yes sir, E," Marz said, grinning.

The guy smiled, and it made Nick realize how much Easy had changed in the few months they'd all been back together. A few weeks into their investigation, he'd admitted to them that he'd been badly depressed and battling suicidal thoughts. They'd all been gutted to know how bad Easy had been silently struggling, but they'd banded together around him, and Shane and Emilie had made sure he'd gotten the medicine and therapy he'd needed to fight the demons in his head. "Here's to a long life, and a merry one. A quick death, and an easy one. A pretty girl," he said with a wink at Nick, "and a loyal one. A stiff drink, and another one." Another round of bottoms up. At this rate, they were going to lose every dollar they owned at the casino, and Nick didn't give a shit.

"I'm not good at this," Charlie said with a sheepish smile. "But I'll give it a go." Jeremy grinned at him as

Marz clapped him on the back. "To Nick, if you hurt my sister, I'll kill you in your sleep."

For a moment, the words hung there, then everyone burst into guffaws. Yeah, Charlie Merritt fit in just fine.

"No worries. I'll fucking drink to that, Charlie," Nick said, laughing. He took a big gulp of whiskey, enjoying the bite as it went down. "Okay, I've got something to say. First, to nights and friends I'll never forget." Holding his glass high, he looked each man in the eye. "And second, to our enemies."

"*Fuck you!*" they all called out.

"Amen," Nick said. But tonight wasn't a night to worry about enemies. Tonight was a night for celebrating the good things in life. And if Becca hadn't already done it, being with all these guys was making him realize exactly how much good Nick had.

"Ooh, I HAVE a fun idea," Kat said, pulling out her phone. "Everyone take either a cleavage shot or an upskirt shot and text it to your guy. Make 'em remember what they're missing out on tonight." She tugged down the V-neck of her emerald green satin dress and took a picture of herself. A few flicks of her fingers, and she said, "There. Go on, now. Make 'em sweat."

Becca could only laugh as she lifted her skirt and took a picture of the virginal white panties she wore, complete with glittering sequins. They'd made her feel very bridal. "I love this idea," she said, shooting off a text to Nick. Then again, she'd already been three glasses of champagne into Happyville before they'd left the restaurant, and Kat had given her a fourth when she'd gotten into the limo. So she was prone to love just about any idea just then. "Ooh, I'm sending Nick one of each so he can see how beautiful this necklace is on me," she said, taking a shot down the top of her dress but making sure to get the incredible yellow diamond sun-shaped pendant he'd given her into the frame. She loved him so freaking much.

"Oh, my God," Sara said. "I have no cleavage to speak of, people. But Shane did like these red panties I have on." Awkwardly and with a lot of blushing, she managed to take a picture up the skirt of her little red dress. "You, on the other hand, have great boobs, Jenna," she said to her sister.

"I already sent mine," Jenna said, looking very pleased with herself. She'd worn a form-fitting black dress that gave her the most enviable hourglass shape. On Becca's last day off, they'd gone shopping for new dresses for tonight and the rehearsal dinner, and all the time Becca had gotten to spend with these women was making her fall in love with them even more. She had women she was friendly with at the hospital, but it had been since nursing school that she'd last had truly close friends. Best friends. Now she had four of them.

"I need help with mine," Emilie said, grinning. She handed her phone to Kat, who sat next to her. Laughing, Emilie turned and got on all fours on the seat. She pulled up the bottom of her gold dress just enough to reveal a really tiny pair of satin black panties.

"I knew I liked you," Kat said, taking the picture. "And why am I not surprised that Derek is an ass man?"

"Oh, my. This is going to be a night of TMI, isn't it?" Sara asked, sipping at her champagne.

"Yes," Emilie said, sitting down again. "But if I've discovered anything, it's that life is too damn short and uncertain to hold back."

"I'll drink to that," Becca said, draining her glass.

And that's when all their phones started blowing up. Laughter filled the limo as they all read the guys' reactions to their selfies. Becca couldn't stop grinning—or fantasizing—about Nick's reply.

I'm going to tear those fucking things off with my teeth. Count on it.

His reply to her second selfie made her all warm inside.

You are so beautiful. My sunshine.

"Okay, as much as I want to get you drunk, I also don't want to see you sick." Kat handed Becca a bottle of water and grabbed one for herself. "Drink this before you have any more champagne."

"I will. But why aren't you drinking?" Becca asked. Kat hadn't touched her champagne at dinner, and she was the only one of them without a drink now.

"So I can take care of you," Kat said. "Besides, I'm naturally high on life. Runs in the family. Well, at least with Jeremy and me, anyway."

Becca laughed. Kat and Nick were alike in so many ways, and their stubbornness often had them butting heads. By the time the limo pulled to a stop, Becca had dutifully followed orders and emptied the bottle. "I'm so excited to see what we're doing," she said. The girls had insisted on keeping it a secret.

The driver, an older man named Tony, whose military bearing reminded Becca of her father, opened the door. They spilled out onto the street, and Kat wrapped her arm through Becca's as they walked up to the doors of a posh salon and spa. "We're getting completely pampered. Anything you want. The places is all ours for the night."

"Oh, my God," Becca said. "This is the coolest thing ever." And she didn't know the half of it until they were inside. There was more champagne, a table full of chocolate-covered strawberries and Godiva truffles, and a mountain of presents.

"You never got to have a shower," Emilie said. "So consider tonight your combination shower and bachelorette party."

Becca was completely overwhelmed by the thoughtfulness and perfection of the whole thing. "You shouldn't have done all this," she said. "But I'm really, really glad you did."

They all traded their dresses and heels for robes and slippers and settled in for pedicures. One of the ladies from the spa kept Becca in a continuous stream of drinks and treats and presents. So many presents. A gorgeous lingerie set for her wedding night. A big basket of body lotions and spa products and makeup. A set of pillow cases that read *Mr. Right* and *Mrs. Always Right*. A trio of crystal picture frames. A happily ever after wish jar with their names on it to be put out for people to fill at their wedding. A pair of red satin panties with the words *You got lucky* on the crotch. Sparkling, drop diamond earrings. A beautiful framed print that had Becca and Nick's names, their wedding date, and the words *And they lived happily ever after.*

"I love everything so much," Becca said as the woman put the finishing touches on her purple toe polish. "Not that long ago, I had almost no one in my life. My parents were gone. Charlie had distanced himself. And I threw myself into work just to fill the void. Now, I can't believe everything I have. I'm so grateful for each and every one of you."

"I've never had friends like this before," Sara said, blinking fast. "Sometimes I'm afraid that I'm dreaming and I'll wake up."

"It's not a dream, Sara," Jenna said. "What happened is that you woke up from the nightmare. *This* is your reality now."

"Oh, God, you guys are going to make me cry," Emilie said. "I think we need more champagne. And chocolate."

Kat's pedicure was already done, so she brought the bottle around and refilled everyone's glasses. In all, Becca was treated to a pedicure, a manicure, and a mini facial, and she had her eyebrows shaped. She hadn't felt so relaxed in forever. No doubt everything Nick had learned earlier in the day helped, and for the first time since she'd returned to work, she felt hopeful.

It was after eleven by the time they were all dressed again and had the presents and leftovers packed up to take home. Tony carried everything out to the Hummer for them, then Becca noticed him talking quietly with Kat.

"Is everything okay?" Becca asked, joining them at the front door of the spa.

"Yes, Miss Merritt," Tony said. "There's a man hanging around down the block who's drunk and belligerent. He threw a bottle at a passing car earlier. And he gave me a little bit of guff when I asked him to move away from the Hummer. He left without incident, but I don't want any of you stepping outside until we're ready to get in the vehicle and depart."

Through the haze of champagne and sugar, Becca's gut clenched. "Okay, of course."

"Don't worry," Kat said. "It's just a precaution."

When the other women emerged from the bathroom, Tony said, "Ladies, I'd like you to move directly into the limo once you're outside, please." He went out first, paused as he opened the door, and waved them out.

A half block down the street, a tall, thin man wearing too-big pants and an oversized black hoodie with the hood up skulked in a circle, his arms waving and his body gesticulating like he was having an argument. From this distance, Becca couldn't make out the man's face, but she couldn't deny the relief she felt at the fact that the man was way too thin to be Woodson, who'd been bulky and muscular. Not that she should be worrying about Woodson. Nick's research today really had made her feel a lot better.

Kat bustled Becca into the limo, then climbed in after.

As the other women got in, Becca could just make out the man shouting.

"You think you so fucking better than me!" he yelled, his voice full of drunken slur. "Well, you not! You not! And I'm gonna show you! I'm gonna show you!"

The minute Emilie was in, Tony had the door secured behind them, cutting off the rest of the tirade. Almost immediately, the engine started and the Hummer eased away from the curb.

"Please don't let that tarnish your night," Kat said.

Becca smiled. "Not at all. Nothing could tarnish this night. It was fantastic. Perfect. One of the best ever." She meant it, too. And the whipped cream on her cake? In just a few minutes, it would be midnight. And that meant in just one week, Becca was going to be married to the love of her life.

And absolutely nothing could ruin the amazing miracle of that.

Chapter Nine

"NICK," CHEN SAID when he called on Wednesday morning. "I've got bad news."

"Shit, what is it?" Nick asked. When a guy like Chen said he had bad news, you knew it was *bad*.

From the driver's seat of his truck, Shane frowned, his expression full of questions. He parked the truck in front of the dry cleaner. They'd dropped Becca off at work a half hour before and were picking up their uniforms for the wedding.

"Woodson's in Baltimore. Has been for at least a week, maybe longer."

Nick's gut dropped to the floor, his mind racing. A week? That meant he'd been in town long enough to be responsible for the stuffed animal, for Becca's feeling of being watched at the mall, and maybe even for some of her sightings that they'd thought were impossible and chalked up to her PTSD. "Goddamnit. Are you sure? How do you know?"

"I put a guy on the ground in South Carolina. He learned from some locals that Woodson had left town and traded vehicles with his uncle. I managed to track the uncle's truck to a rest stop near Richmond, where another car had been reported stolen. That car was found abandoned in Baltimore County last week, which we just put together. Otherwise, the guy's been way off the grid. No credit cards. No known vehicles. I have two undercover agents in the city looking for him from within the gang scene. As soon as we locate him, we'll grab him."

"Fuck," Nick said, the weight of this new development crushing in on him. "Thanks for letting me know. Keep me posted." They hung up. "Head back to the hospital. Now," Nick said.

Shane had the truck in reverse and barreling out of the parking lot immediately. "Talk to me."

"Woodson's in town. Has been for over a week. We got fucking outfoxed." Nick dialed Becca. It went to voice mail. "Please call me as soon as you get this, Becca." Ice sloshed into his gut as Nick filled Shane in.

"No one stays off the grid like that unless they fear they're being hunted. Or they don't want to be noticed," Shane said, running the tail end of a yellow light.

Nick appreciated the hell out of his friend's aggressive driving. He really did. "Given the situation in the city, it's probably some of both in this case. But I'm a helluva lot more worried about the latter."

"Roger that," Shane said, darting around other cars as much as he could.

Nick tried Becca's cell again. Voice mail. Damnit. He was about ready to crawl out of his skin. Flipping through the contacts on his phone, he found the number for Barry Coleman at the hospital.

"Mr. Coleman, this is Nick Rixey, Becca Merritt's fiancé," Nick said, his knee bouncing as he scanned his gaze over the street as it flew by.

"Nick, what can I do for you?"

"I need you to find Becca and keep an eye on her until I get there. She's not answering her cell, but I know she might be with a patient. I just got word that Tyrell Woodson is back in town and has been for more than a week. Since we still don't know who pulled the stunt with the stuffed animal, I'd feel better if Becca left early today until we get to the bottom of this and know what Woodson's up to. It seems he took some pains to get back into the city unnoticed."

"I wish I had your connections for intel," Coleman said.

"Yeah, well I wish I didn't need them."

"I hear you," the other man said. "I'll find Becca and stay with her until you get here." They hung up.

In another five minutes, Nick and Shane made it back to the hospital. Nick barely waited for Shane to bring the truck to a stop before he was opening the door. "Pick us up near the ER entrance. It's more sheltered."

"You got it," Shane said.

Nick rushed across the plaza to the main entrance, his gaze scanning the streetscape, the crowd, the sea of faces. He let his guard down for five goddamned seconds, and this was what happened. Becca, potentially exposed to danger and completely unaware.

Inside, he made his way to Coleman's office. Relief flooded through him.

Becca. Sitting across from Coleman at his desk. Her face was a shade too pale, but otherwise she was safe, sound, a fucking sight for sore eyes.

"Nick," she said, rising as soon as she saw him. "He's back?"

Nick cupped her face in his hands. "Yes, but Chen's on it. Woodson won't be free for long. Don't worry, okay?"

She gave him a doubtful look that was like a knife to the gut.

Nick turned to Coleman. "Thanks for your help." They shook hands.

"Anything else you need, you just let me know," the man said.

Taking Becca's hand in his, Nick led her to the main ER entrance, keeping back from the glass until he saw Shane's big black truck pull into the drop-off lane. "That's our ride. Come on."

They jogged toward the truck, Nick's gaze doing a constant scanning circuit as they moved. He got Becca into the truck's backseat, shut her door, and moved to his own—which was when his eye caught it. A glint of morning sun off metal. There at the corner of the building.

Nick opened the passenger door just in time, the report of the gunfire reaching his ears only a second before the round pinged off the door. Close. Too damn close. He dove into the cab. "Go, go!"

"Fuck!" Shane punched the accelerator and pulled the truck into a hard U-ey. Another round hit the back quarter panel.

"Get down, Becca," Nick said as he reached for the Glock at the small of his back. But she was way ahead of him, tucked in a ball on the floor behind his seat. He didn't have a clear shot of anything, especially with chaos already breaking out around the ER's entrance as people dove for cover and the couple of on-site police officers rushed into defensive positions.

In what felt like long minutes but was only a few seconds, they were clear of the area. Shane ran a red light to get them away from the hospital altogether.

Twisting in his seat, Nick looked out the cab's rear window. "Watch for a tail."

"On it," Shane said. "You need to alert the team, Vance, Chen."

"Yeah," Nick said, but first he needed to check on Becca. Christ, every reassurance he'd offered the past week had just been blown to shit. His gut was a wreck, his mind unhelpfully crafting one horror story after another about what might've happened if Chen hadn't called. Or if Nick hadn't returned to the hospital immediately. Or if Coleman hadn't been able to pull Becca off the floor. "Becca, are you okay?"

"I don't know," she said, her voice shaky. When she looked up at him, her skin was ashen.

He reached back and clutched her hand as he dialed Marz.

"Yo, hoss, wassup?" Marz said.

"We've got a situation," Nick said, filling him in. "Let everyone know what's going on. And if you have a chance, scan the security feeds around our neighborhood looking for anything potentially suspicious. We've been keeping an eye out for the wrong damn car."

"You got it," Marz said.

Nick had just hung up when his cell rang again. Chen. Nick put it on speaker.

"I heard about the hospital. You okay?" Chen asked by way of a greeting. Nick wasn't surprised that Chen had information that was only minutes old.

"Yeah, we're in one piece," Nick said. "But it was fucking close. Too close."

"Damnit. Wanted to let you know we have a lead on where Woodson's been staying. Putting together a raid for tonight as we speak."

"Well there's a bit of good news," Nick said. "You need backup?"

"No, you stay hunkered down. I'll let you know when it's done."

"I need you to take this guy out," Nick said, anger lancing through the words. If it had just been him in danger, it would have been one thing. But now it was Becca. Now it was *his family*. And that was a whole other goddamned thing. "I need this situation to go the fuck away."

"I hear you," Chen said. "And I'm working on it." He clicked off.

"If anyone can take care of this, Chen can, right?" Becca asked from the backseat. A little color had returned to her cheeks.

"Yes," Nick and Shane both said at the same time.

When they got back to Hard Ink, Marz had everyone else assembled and briefed in the big unfinished space across from their apartment that was part gym, part war room. It was where they'd run the whole of their investigation against the Church Gang and the mercenaries who'd killed Becca's father and smuggled heroin from Afghanistan into Baltimore. Nick wasn't thrilled at all about the similarity of this meeting to the many they'd held during the investigation they'd thought was done. Closed. Behind them once and for all.

Except it wasn't. Because sometimes the past wouldn't fucking die.

"Chen's people think they've discovered where Woodson has been holing up. They're going after him tonight. His actions at the hospital demonstrate his intention to get revenge, so until we hear from Chen, we're back on lockdown again. I don't want anyone leaving the building today," Nick said.

"What if they don't get him?" Becca asked from where she sat on a folding chair near Marz's improvised desk.

The other team members traded looks with Nick. "I don't know the answer to that yet," Nick said.

Becca nodded. "Do we need to think about postponing the wedding?"

The question was like a punch to the gut, especially because he'd been asking himself the same thing. Fuck.

"Not yet," Nick said. A bleak sadness filled Becca's baby blues, and the fact that this scumbag had managed to hurt her yet again lanced boiling hot rage through his blood. Enough was efuckingnough.

The meeting broke up, and the day crawled by like an inchworm moving in reverse.

Nick spent hours worshipping every inch of Becca's body, hoping to keep them both distracted from everything that was at stake as long as he could. The women made six batches of homemade chocolate chip cookies. They watched movies until they were all cross-eyed. And still it wasn't time for the raid.

Finally, a little after ten o'clock, Nick's cell rang with a call from Chen. The devastating news was that they'd apprehended a number of former Churchmen—but Woodson hadn't been among them.

"Well, what's next?" Nick barked into the phone. "This guy came after Becca three times. He's not going to stop."

"I know, Nick," Chen said. "We're interrogating the Churchmen we brought in. We'll find him."

But how fast would they find him? And would Chen find Woodson before Woodson found Becca again?

Because Nick would never survive if something happened to the only woman he'd ever loved.

Chapter Ten

CHEN SHOWED UP at Hard Ink Friday morning. His people still hadn't caught Woodson. And Becca was beside herself. She couldn't believe . . . so many things. That Woodson was back. That they might have to cancel the wedding. That maybe she really had seen Woodson some of the times she'd chalked it up to her imagination.

The whole group gathered in the gym, and Chen sat in the middle of them, wearing his usual, nondescript khaki pants and light blue button-down. Chen wasn't his real name, but it was the only one they knew him by—the one that had been on the nametag fastened to the stolen doctor's coat Chen had been wearing the first time Nick had seen him. They'd been at the hospital where Jeremy and Kat had been treated after the funeral.

"I have a proposal for dealing with Woodson," Chen said, scanning the group and finally settling his gaze on Nick and Becca.

"Let's hear it," Nick said.

"I get the word out on the street that Becca is going to be at the restaurant tonight for her rehearsal dinner. We lure Woodson to us rather than wait for him to come at you." Chen's matter-of-fact words hung there for a long moment.

"No," Nick said. Just as matter-of-factly.

This wasn't the first time it had ever been proposed that they use Becca as bait. Nor was it the first time Nick had reacted negatively to the idea. "Nick, Becca said."

"No, Becca. We've been there, done that, and you got hurt," he said. The fierce protectiveness in his gaze made her love him even more.

"I know, but the last time, we also caught Woodson and got information out of him that saved Charlie's life. So it worked," she said. Tension hung so thick in the room you could cut it with a knife. "The alternative is that we cancel the wedding, stay shut up inside the building, and wait it out, right?"

Chen nodded. "We will get him. It's a matter of when, not if."

"I believe you," Becca said. "But when kinda matters a lot right now. The wedding can be rescheduled if we need to, of course, but none of us wants this hanging over our heads. If we can end it tonight, let's end it."

"I agree," Kat said, looking at Nick with sympathy in her eyes.

"So do I," Beckett said. "We'll all be there. We'll all be armed. Nothing's going to happen to Becca or anyone else."

"And my team will be there," Chen said.

"Is this what everyone thinks?" Nick asked, his voice like gravel. He crossed his arms and surveyed the group. Nods and affirmatives all around. "Fuck. Then what's the plan? Because I want it to be goddamned foolproof."

For the next hour, the guys strategized. Chen had brought plans for the Italian restaurant where they were scheduled to go, as well as a big map of the surrounding streets and alleys. He'd arranged to have surveillance on the restaurant starting immediately, to make sure no one arrived early and found a place to lay in wait. When they were done, Chen put in calls to his undercover contacts to get the word out. He was apparently confident enough in the way information moved within and between gangs to think that the word would make it to Woodson in time if in fact he was actively looking for her. Worst-case scenario, it didn't, and he didn't show. And then they were right back to square one, but no further behind.

After Chen left, Becca turned to Nick, where they were all still gathered in the gym. "I want to be armed tonight."

"Me too," Kat said.

Nick and Beckett traded a look, but then Nick nodded. "Everyone who's comfortable handling a weapon should be armed. I want redundancies on top of redundancies where safety is concerned. And for the record, I fucking hate this."

Becca wrapped her arms around Nick and laid her head against his chest. "I do, too. But I hate being scared more."

Nodding, Nick said, "I've got a few calls I want to make. But then I'll be wrapped up here."

"Okay," Becca said. "Maybe I'll go throw together some lunch for everyone." Staying busy was the best way to keep from going crazy. At least, it had worked for her during the team's investigation. No reason why it shouldn't now.

"I'll help," Emilie said.

"Me too," Sara said.

In the end, all four women made their way back to the apartment with Becca, and she appreciated the silent show of support. She really did. They decided on tacos, and everyone got to work chopping veggies and browning the meat. Emilie apparently made a mean spicy Spanish rice, so she took charge of that.

As Becca stood at the stove, the whole thing suddenly crashed over her like a tidal wave. The shooting at the hospital. Knowing everyone would be in danger tonight. The prospect of facing Woodson again—for real this time. "Can you watch this?" Becca asked Emilie, laying down the big spoon with which she'd been stirring the ground beef. "I'll be right back."

She rushed down the hallway and ducked into Kat's sometimes-room rather than her own—the one she shared with Nick. First, because she wanted to be alone in case Nick returned from making his calls. Second, because her wedding gown was in this room, hanging on the outside of the closet door. Luckily, they'd picked up their dresses from the bridal boutique before the lockdown had started, and now it was here waiting for her.

For whenever Nick and Becca were finally able to get

married. Because her gut told her it wasn't going to be tomorrow.

Becca sagged down onto the edge of the mattress, her gaze drinking in the gleaming white satin and the sparkling beadwork at the waist. Her lip quivered and her eyes pricked, but she wasn't giving in to tears. She was done crying. Now she was just fucking angry.

It doesn't matter, Becca. The wedding is just one day in a forever that lasts the rest of your life. It's just one day.

And it was. She knew it. But their love had overcome big obstacles—Nick's initial belief that her father had betrayed him, sophisticated and numerous enemies, multiple attempts on their lives. What they had was hard-fought and well-earned. They *deserved* a day of celebration and happily ever afters.

Two soft knocks sounded against the door.

Becca straightened her back, took a deep breath, and said, "Come in."

"Hey," Kat said, leaning in the doorway. "Can I join you?"

"It's your room," Becca said with a small smile.

Kat shut the door and sat down on the bed next to Becca. "It really is an amazing gown. Nick is going to swallow his tongue when he sees you in it."

It might've been the first time all day Becca smiled. "I am looking forward to seeing him see me in it for the first time."

Grasping her hand, Kat nailed her with that Rixey stare. "You just have to hang in for a few more hours. This is almost over."

"I know," Becca said. "I know. But is it bad that I want to be the one to end this asshole's life once and for all? I just want to see the consciousness bleed out of his eyes so I can know it's over for good."

"Not even a little bad," Kat said. "You guys deserve a happily ever after."

Becca chuffed out a humorless laugh. "We all do. But sometimes I'm afraid all we're going to get is . . . a hard ever after. You know?"

Kat's gaze was full of determination. "This guy's going down one way or the other, Becca. And besides, a hard ever after sounds like it could be good to me. I mean, *you know*, hard can be good."

That eked a smile out of Becca, and that smile turned into a chuckle. "Yeah, hard can be good."

"No," Kat said, grinning now. "Hard *is* good. Really fucking good."

It was stupid and childish and ridiculous, but as the hard jokes started flowing out of them, they descended into outright crying giggles and really unattractive snorting that was a helluva better release than tears could ever be.

"Thank you," Becca finally managed. "I really needed that."

"Good. Now come on, let's go eat." Kat pulled her up from the bed.

"I'll catch up," Becca said. "Need to use the bathroom." She headed back toward her room, passing Shane and Sara's on the way. Their door was open, and something caught Becca's eye. She stepped back to the opening and peered in at Shane's big medic case just inside the doorway. Becca shut herself inside the room, knelt, and opened the lid to the case.

When her gaze finally landed on a bottle of injectable diazepam, an idea came to mind. Nick wanted redundancies upon redundancies; well, this certainly fit. And given that Woodson had gotten his hands on her twice before, she wanted a way to hurt him up close if it happened again. Without letting herself question what was probably a totally useless idea, she filled a syringe with a dose guaranteed to induce sleep in a man Woodson's size. Quickly, she put everything away and tucked the syringe into the pocket of her dress, which hung in Nick's closet. No one even had to know the syringe was there.

One thing was for sure, Becca Merritt was done feeling like a victim. She was ready to fight for this life she wanted, once and for freaking all.

THEY ARRIVED AT the inn early for the rehearsal. Before Becca even stepped foot out of the stretch Hummer, Nick wanted to take a look around and discuss a plan with the security he'd brought in extra for the rehearsal. This was the same team who'd be running things at the wedding, so they already understood the nature of the threat from when he'd met with them earlier. To add another layer of security, Chen had arranged to put agents from his detail at either end of the long block on which the inn sat, providing an effective roadblock and a defensive perimeter.

It was all likely overkill. Nick knew it was. The bait

would lure Woodson to the restaurant, not here. Hell, they hadn't even published a wedding announcement, so the details of their arrangements could only be known by people with whom they'd shared invitations.

When he was satisfied, he opened the door to the ladies' limousine. "Let's practice us a wedding," he said with a smile. He might be tense as hell inside, but he didn't want to do anything—well, anything *more* than what had to be done—to take away from the joy of the occasion. Becca deserved a happily ever after, and Nick was determined to give her one. No matter what it took.

Becca stepped out of the limo in a stunning long blue dress that made the color of her eyes almost glow. She adjusted the long decorative chain of her purse on her shoulder. He'd given her a small handgun that would fit the bag, and even though she knew how to use it—thanks to her father—Nick really fucking hoped she never had to. But he couldn't have agreed more that she should have the protection on her. It was *always* wise to be prepared for a snafu, that was for damn sure.

Sonya greeted them at the gatehouse and guided the group of them inside. The first floor of the inn was where the cocktail party immediately after the ceremony would take place while they were taking wedding photographs. A tall round table filled with champagne flutes stood in the center of the floor. "Please help yourself while you wait for the minister to arrive."

"Do you want to see the upstairs where we'll hold the reception?" Becca asked the women.

Even though the security team had assured them

that the house had been locked up tight all day, with no one coming or going until they and Sonya had arrived to open up for their rehearsal, Nick wasn't comfortable letting Becca go alone. In the end, everyone went along for the tour. It really was a nice place. The kind of place where happy memories were made. Nick wanted that for Becca. For both of them.

They didn't have to wait long for the chaplain to arrive. Nick didn't know the man personally, but Thomas McAdams was a military chaplain who was a friend of a friend, which was how they'd managed to book him on such short notice. Nick guessed that McAdams was not much older than he was, and the chaplain seemed eager and interested and kind. Nick immediately liked him.

McAdams greeted the whole wedding party, then Sonya gave him a general tour of the outdoor space where the ceremony would take place. They'd process up the brick-lined courtyard between chairs that were already set up for them, and the ceremony itself would take place on a raised brick patio against the backdrop of the rear of the gorgeous Carroll Mansion. A plain wide wooden arch stood there now. Tomorrow it would be decorated with flowers.

As Sonya, McAdams, and Becca spoke, Nick couldn't help but be on the alert. His eyes and ears were wide open, despite the fact that things were quiet. Exactly as they should be. And he wasn't the only one. Every one of his teammates had their game faces on. Nick was fucking glad.

"Okay, now that I have the lay of the land," McAdams said, "I'd like to go over what you all indicated you wanted for the ceremony. Then we'll walk through it as a group, and I'll show you where to walk and stand, all that sort of thing. And then we'll do an actual dry run, music and all if you have it."

"I have it on my phone," Becca said.

"That'll work," McAdams said. For a few moments, they discussed vows, wording for various parts of the ceremony, who was holding the rings, and how they wanted him to introduce them to the audience when the ceremony was complete. "Okay, let's walk through it all. Anyone should feel free to interrupt this time with questions or suggestions. In fact, *now* is the main time to ask questions," he said. "Becca, where do you want to start the procession from?"

Sonya stepped forward. "If I might make a suggestion," she said, guiding them back into the first floor of the inn. In the back corner, there were three doors. "There are two private party rooms here we've set up for the bridal party to use before the ceremony." She let them into one and turned on the lights. The rectangular room had a long table that seated eight in the center, with old-fashioned leather armchairs clustered in groupings along one wall. A floor-to-ceiling mirror hung at the far end of the room. "Both rooms are identical. These usually work nicely to allow for last-minute preparations, privacy if the bride doesn't want to be seen by the groom beforehand, and staging for the ceremony itself."

"Yes, that's what we'd discussed. I don't want him to see me until I'm walking down the aisle," Becca said, smiling at him. Nick couldn't fucking wait. "So then we'd be processing from inside?"

"That's right," Sonya said, leading them back out to the main room. "The groomsmen will join Nick at the dais ahead of time. We'll keep these doors shut until it's time for the women to walk. When the music changes, we'll open the doors and the bridesmaids will go one by one. And then the music will change again to whatever song Becca has chosen to walk to, and she'll proceed as well. Is someone walking you down the aisle, Becca?"

"Oh." Without hesitation, she turned to Charlie. "Will you? Please?"

Her brother's face filled with emotion. "Yeah. Of course."

Becca pressed a kiss to Charlie's face. "Thank you. I'm sorry that in all the craziness I didn't think of this sooner." He shook his head, clearly moved by her request.

"Very good," McAdams said. "Let's head outside to see how we'll arrange things at the dais."

As they walked the length of the courtyard, Sonya said, "Remember not to walk too fast, bridesmaids. It's longer than usual, so everyone always wants to run up the aisle." The women all laughed. When they got to the raised brick porch, Sonya directed each of them to where they should stand for the ceremony itself.

After that, McAdams sped them through the words so they knew what would happen. And then Sonya was guiding them back down the aisle again to show them where to stand for the reception line they were going to form before returning to the porch for group pictures.

This all seemed pretty basic to Nick, and frankly he was a little impatient with it. But that was just the broader situation talking. He tried to block it out as much as he could, especially since Becca seemed to be enjoying herself. And given what they were yet to face at dinner, he didn't want to do anything to ruin that.

"Okay, let's do a full run-through," McAdams said. "Gentlemen, except Charlie, come with me."

Nick frowned and turned to Becca.

She smiled and winked. "Go ahead. I'll be right there."

He gave her a quick kiss. "You're already the prettiest bride there ever was."

"Aw, sweet man. I don't care what anyone says, I'm going to run up this aisle to you," she said as he headed for the door.

"I won't object to that at all," he called over his shoulder as he made his way toward the mansion.

And then Sonya guided the women back inside and closed the doors behind them.

Chapter Eleven

"THIS IS SO exciting, Becca," Sara said, looking around at the elegant room. "This place is so gorgeous."

"I know. I fell in love immediately," Becca said. The beautiful summer night, the sweet fragrance of the garden flowers, the ambiance provided by the historic architecture. Tomorrow was going to be amazing.

Assuming it happened.

No, it *was* happening. Becca just had to believe it.

"Becca," Sonya said. "If you have your phone, I can hook it up to the sound system so it plays in the courtyard. Just show me what songs you want."

Becca opened her wedding playlist. "This is the music that can play while people are being seated," Becca said, pointing to a list of songs. "This one is for the bridesmaids' procession, and this one is for mine."

"Very good." Sonya hooked up the phone. Classical music immediately filtered in from outside. Sonya had Becca line the women up in the order in which she wanted them to march, and the music changed for the bridesmaids. "And now we're marching," Sonya said as she opened the doors. The warm twilight air spilled in. White lights twinkled in the trees and on lines strung across the courtyard. It was magical.

One by one, the women walked out the doors. Jenna, Sara, Emilie, then Kat. And then it was just Becca and Charlie left to walk down the aisle. She turned to him. "I'm so lucky to have you as my brother, Charlie. I just want you to know how grateful I am that all of this has brought us closer again." Next to finding Nick, that was one of the brightest silver linings in everything that had happened.

He gave her a small smile. "I feel the same exact way," he said.

"Okay," Sonya said from beside the doors. "Now I'll change to the wedding march, and it'll be your turn."

"Shut the fucking door," came a deep voice from behind them.

Becca whirled. She recognized the voice immediately. Woodson. For real this time.

"Who are you, sir?" Sonya asked. "You can't be in here."

He brandished a gun directly at her. "I *said*, shut the fucking door. Now."

As the blood drained from her face, Sonya hastily pushed the doors closed.

Becca fumbled for her purse, but the decorative metal clasp stuck.

"Don't move, Becca. Don't even fucking breathe. In fact, toss that bag down. Now." Woodson stalked closer.

Which was when Becca realized he'd lost *a lot* of weight since she'd seen him two months ago. His eyes and face had the sunken, haggard look of an addict. He'd let his hair grow back in, too. He was no longer bald. "It was you. On the street the other night."

"Told you I was gonna show you. And when I found out about your wedding, I thought, what better time. Was gonna wait 'til tomorrow. Do it up right for the big crowd. But I figure, I got you now for sure."

Charlie moved just the smallest amount to angle himself in front of her, and Woodson tracked the movement like a hawk. He trained his weapon at Charlie's head and arched an eyebrow. "Get down on the floor," he ordered Becca's brother. "You, too." He glared at Sonya, who rushed to comply. Charlie sank down more slowly, and Becca could feel the anger and frustration rolling off of him.

Becca needed to distract Woodson from whatever he planned to do. Delay him, at the very least. At some point Nick was going to realize something was wrong—she had faith in that into her very bones. He wouldn't let anything happen to her. So she just had to hold on for a short while.

"I told you to drop the bag. Do it *now*," Woodson barked out, punctuating his words by jabbing the gun at the air.

Her belly sinking, Becca dropped the purse next to her feet.

Woodson gave her a droll stare. "Don't fucking play me. Kick it away."

She did, a little of her hope going with it as it slid across the hardwood floor. "How did you know about my wedding?" she asked, wanting to keep him talking.

"Yeah, that was some lucky shit, wasn't it? For me, anyway." He stalked closer, slowly, like he was paranoid despite the fact that he was the one with the weapon. "Little sister of a Churchman who was killed works in housekeeping at the hospital. Guess someone left an invitation out in the staff break room."

"So she's how you got the stuffed animal in to me," she said, her voice shaky. She hadn't been freaking out for nothing after all. Woodson really had been lurking around the edges of her life. For how long she wasn't sure. But what a lesson to trust her instincts.

His grin was sadistic and cruel. "Enjoyed my little calling card, did ya?" He didn't give her the chance to answer, because as soon as he was close enough, he roughly grabbed her arm and tugged her against him. He spun her so her back was to his front, then he dragged her away from Charlie's reach. His forearm pressed savagely into her throat, choking her as she struggled to keep her heels under her. "Because of you," he hissed into her ear, "I lost everything I had. And now you're going to see how that feels, starting with him."

Woodson lifted the gun.

Becca had to do some—

The syringe!

In her rage and terror, it seemed to her that he moved

in slow motion. And that she did, too. An eternity seemed to pass as he took aim and she reached into the pocket of her maxi dress. Uncapped the syringe. Jabbed it into Woodson's thigh.

The world froze for an eternity.

Woodson shouted.

The gun fired.

She stumbled as he did, his arm still squeezing her throat.

And then she was falling, falling backward with him, as the gun fired again.

NICK WATCHED AS the women made their way up the aisle. When Kat got closer, she grinned and made a face at him, but then her gaze shifted to his left. To Beckett. And hell if the look his sister was giving his friend wasn't how Becca sometimes looked at Nick. For as much as Nick had been thrown by Beckett's interest in Kat, the two of them had proven to be damn good for each other.

As Kat took her place, Nick searched for Becca. And found the doors to the first floor closed again. He frowned. Maybe it was to allow the bride to make a grand entrance once the wedding march began? Nick stretched his neck and rolled his shoulders. Probably made him an asshole, but he really wanted this rehearsal to be over.

He stared at the doors. The same music continued on. A prickle ran over his scalp. He looked to his teammates, standing at his left. But his gut had already decided. "I don't like this." No, more than that. "Something's fucking wrong."

The men took off as a unit. "Kat, get everyone in the limo and keep them there," Nick heard Beckett say. "Go."

Becca. Jesus Christ, Becca. Where are you?

Nick full out sprinted down the courtyard. Two security guards spilled out from the gatehouse and filled in behind them.

"Go around to the side and take the shot through a window if you have it," Nick called. Easy and Marz broke off. Guns in hand, the remaining three slowed as they approached the doors. Curtains covered the glass, keeping Nick from seeing inside. In a quiet jog, they hugged the building as they got closer, then Nick used hand signals to communicate the plan. Him on one side, Beckett and Marz on the other. Beckett would force entry, Marz would provide sweeping cover and fire, and Nick would take out the target—assuming he had a shot. There were three friendlies inside.

It was the only way he could think of Becca as his brain shifted to ice-cold operational mode.

Gunfire. One shot. Then another.

And it didn't fucking sound like it had come from the exterior of the building. It had come from inside.

No! Not Becca! Not my sunshine!

With a violent kick, Beckett exploded open the doors. A scream from inside.

Nick swept in to witness something he would never forget for the rest of his life. Becca on the floor on top of Woodson. She wrestled a gun away from him, then rose on stumbling, unsure feet, the gun trained right at the man's head.

Nick didn't know whether to be terrified, proud, or completely fucking dumbfounded.

Gun trained on Woodson, Nick slowly came around so he had a clear view of the man and of Becca's face.

"Becca, are you okay?" Nick asked, his heart a goddamned freight train in his chest. Seriously. The adrenaline coursing through him was strong enough to knock him off his feet, and as strong as the relief he felt at seeing Becca on hers. But she didn't seem to hear him. "Becca."

"I should kill you," she said, the tone of her voice something he'd never heard before. "I should." Despite the shudders racking her body, she gripped the weapon stably, competently. Her finger sat on the trigger.

Nick glanced to Woodson to find him unconscious, then all his focus narrowed in on her, even as his teammates moved around the room. Still vigilant, Nick moved closer. "Becca, it's me. It's over."

She shook her head. "I *should*," she said again, her face crumpling.

God, his heart was fucking breaking. "No, you shouldn't. No matter how much he deserves it, you don't want a death on your hands. Any death. You don't want that. And I don't want that for you."

Beckett moved around behind Becca, poised to disarm her if he needed to, but Nick gave a single shake of his head.

Nick crouched to force himself closer to her line of sight. "Becca. Sunshine. Look at me."

Shattered blue eyes cut to him, but her gun remained trained on the unconscious man who'd wreaked such havoc on their lives. "Is . . . is Charlie . . ."

"I'm okay," Charlie said, sitting up against the wall by the door. "I'm okay, Becca."

Nick spared a quick glance to her brother. Okay, but hit in the shoulder. Shane was taping gauze to the wound from a kit open on the floor beside him. Jeremy was crouched on Charlie's other side, his head against the guy's good shoulder.

"He's okay?" she asked, like she wasn't quite processing the information.

"Yeah. Charlie's okay. It's all over." Slowly, Nick reached out toward her, his hand gesturing for the gun. "You did so good, Becca. You took Woodson out. You saved Charlie. Let me take it from here." The *how* of it all, Nick didn't yet know, but there was no doubting that Becca had saved this fucking day.

Nick's hand fell on the barrel of the gun. Exerted pressure. Forced it down and away.

Finally, she let it go.

It was like the gun had been holding her up.

Her legs went out beneath her. Beckett was right there and caught her as she sagged to the floor.

Nick was to her in an instant. He handed the gun off to Beckett and took Becca into his arms.

"Charlie," she rasped.

"He's right here," Nick said.

She turned within his embrace, a tortured gasp spilling out of her when she saw her brother. Blood had soaked a crimson circle through the gauze.

"It's just a scratch," Charlie said. "I'm fine."

Movement in the doorway. Chen and his team. "I got here as fast as I could," Chen said. "Are you all okay?"

Hell if Nick knew. "Can you stand?" he asked Becca. He wanted to get her out of there, away from Woodson.

"Yeah," she said as he helped her up. She needed the help. Adrenaline had her shaking like she was freezing, and her teeth were chattering.

Nick shrugged out of his suit coat and wrapped it around her.

"What's that?" Chen asked, pointing at the floor by Woodson's leg.

A syringe.

"Diazepam," Becca said in a weak voice.

"Smart," Chen said in that deadpan way he had.

Not smart. Fucking brilliant. When had she done that?

As they watched, one of Chen's men cuffed Woodson's hands.

"Can we go home?" Becca asked, her voice taking on a flat, odd quality. "I just want to go home."

His arm around her, Nick pulled her in against his chest and stroked her hair. He looked to Shane and Charlie.

"He needs stitches, but not surgery. Went clean through the meat above his collarbone," Shane said.

"Can you fix it up at home?" Charlie asked Shane.

Shane pressed his lips into a tight line. "The job will be neater and less painful if we take you to the hospital."

Shaking his head, Charlie looked from Shane to Nick. "I don't care about that. I want to take Becca home."

"Your call," Nick said to his best friend.

"Okay," Shane said after a moment. "Let's get you up." He and Jeremy both helped Charlie stand.

"He was gonna kill all of you. That was his plan," Becca said out of nowhere.

Chen's gaze swung to Becca, as did several of the other men's. "Did he tell you how he knew to come here?"

"Just that someone in housekeeping at the hospital found one of our wedding invitations and gave it to him," Becca said. Well, that answered some questions right there.

"He came from the basement," Sonya said from where she hovered with her security team at the door.

"We'll get to the bottom of it all," Chen said. "Go home. I'll touch base in a while."

"What's your plan with him?" Nick asked, giving Woodson one last glance.

"The less you know, the better." Chen gave him a pointed look.

Nick knew he didn't have to say anything more, so he just nodded and guided Becca toward the door. "Then let's go home."

Chapter Twelve

BECCA FELT LIKE she was trapped in the dark at the bottom of a well. Somewhere, she knew there was a way out, but as she felt around with blind hands, she couldn't find the ladder. She couldn't find the light.

Despite the fact that, physically, she was functioning.

She answered questions as if by rote. She watched Shane sew up Charlie's wound. She ate part of a piece of pizza that she didn't taste and couldn't finish. She let Nick change her into a pair of pajamas. She felt him touching her, but she couldn't reach him.

She couldn't find the ladder. She couldn't find the light.

But then her friends threw her a rope.

They'd all been sitting around on the couches in the living room for hours, just keeping one another company, just keeping *her* company, when suddenly Kat shot to her feet, her hands fisted, her posture indicating she was waging some great internal debate.

And then she turned to Beckett, who was sitting with his hip resting on the back of the couch behind where she'd been. "I'm pregnant," Kat blurted.

The whole room froze.

Beckett's face was sculpture still. And then his eyes went wide. "Pregnant? Like . . . pregnant?"

"Pregnant like you're going to be a daddy," she said, her voice uncertain.

He came around the couch to her and grasped her face in his hands. And then he gave her a smile that lit up the entire room. "You're pregnant," he whispered, his voice absolutely reverent. One big hand dropped to her stomach. And then he wrapped her in his arms so tightly that it made Kat laugh.

"You're happy," she said.

"I'm terrified," Beckett said. "But I'm also fucking ecstatic."

The whole place erupted in laughter and cheers and words of congratulations, the energy in the room shifting like the planets had just realigned.

Light cracked through the fog clouding Becca's heart and soul.

"I thought I told you there better not be any god-damned children," Nick said.

Kat whirled. "Nick—"

"No, it's okay," Beckett said, his face going serious again.

And then Nick broke out in a deep belly laugh. "I had you. I totally had you." He grasped Beckett's hand and pulled him in for a back-slapping embrace. "Congratulations, man. I'm gonna be the coolest uncle ever. And you're going to be a kick-ass dad."

"Dude, you have no chance of being cooler than me, so give that shit up now," Jeremy said, hugging Kat in beside him.

"You're a fucking asshole," Beckett said as he gave Nick a playful shove. But that million-dollar smile was back on the guy's face again.

"You totally are," Kat said, reaching up to hug Nick next.

Woodenly, Becca rose from the couch to offer her congratulations.

"Well, shit," Marz said from where he stood next to Beckett. "If we're sharing good news, and why the hell not after this day, then I have to tell you that Emilie agreed to marry me this afternoon." He put his arm around her and kissed her on the temple. "And to be honest, I have no idea how I lasted this long without telling you."

"We were going to share it tomorrow at the reception," Emilie said, her voice cracking. "But I'm glad we did it now. We've been dying."

The smiles on the couple's faces were absolutely brilliant with joy. Another round of jubilation erupted.

The rope was in Becca's hands. The light was burning off the fog.

When everyone had a chance to offer congratulations, Sara called out, "I got accepted into college at Johns Hopkins for the fall. I'm going to finish my degree."

Jenna threw her arms around her sister's shoulders. "Oh, that's amazing, Sara. I'm so proud of you."

More celebrations. More light.

Becca could tell the moment her body finally plugged back in, because suddenly she felt *everything*.

"I'm so happy for all of you," she said, her voice strained. "So, so happy."

Tears exploded out of her. Hot, racking, full-body tears. Sobs that had been stored up since the beginning of time.

Someone wrapped her in their arms and sank down to the couch with her. A hand fell on her shoulder. Another on her back. Another on her knees. Someone grasped her hand.

All she had was rope and light now, even though she couldn't rein herself in. The tears felt like they released a poison inside her that had to be purged, so she gave herself over to them. Not that she really had a choice.

Finally, *finally*, she managed a deep, shuddering breath. Tears continued to leak from her eyes, but she could see enough to realize she'd literally soaked Easy with her tears. "I'm sorry," she croaked out.

He shook his head. "Don't you worry about a thing. I got you."

She pressed her hand to his heart. "You're a beautiful, beautiful soul, Easy. I'm so glad you're in my life."

The words visibly impacted him. He gave her hand a squeeze.

Becca turned to the others, who'd all formed a tight circle around her. "I feel that way about each and every one of you. I love you and I cherish you and you're just . . . you're all everything to me." At least she wasn't the only one crying, but she was pretty sure she saw only happy tears.

"We feel the same way about you, Becca," Kat said from where she knelt in front of her.

"Yeah," Marz said. "You're da bomb. Then again, I've thought so since you made a MacGyver reference, so . . ." The men groaned. "What?" Marz asked.

Her heart was so, so full. But something still needed to be said. Urgency flooded through her, and she whirled to face Nick, who'd been sitting behind her, holding her and stroking her back. "I want to marry you. Tomorrow," she said. "Just like we planned. I don't want to wait. I don't want to put it off another second." The words rushed out of her. She scrubbed at her face, despite the fact that her eyes seemed set to non-stop.

Nick grasped her hands. "Becca—"

"Please," she said, sensing that his concern for her was going to push him in the direction of caution, of taking things slow. "The best way to fight back the darkness is with love and light. The best way to cheat death is to live life with no regrets, holding nothing back, just throwing yourself into the messy, vibrant, unexpected beauty of it. *That's* what I want. I don't care about what happened. I refuse to let that win. I don't want to wait to be your always and forever. And for you to be mine."

He studied her face for a long moment, his pale eyes shiny and searching hers. Anticipation hung over the room like a balloon about to burst. "I would love nothing more than to make you my wife. As soon as humanly possible. But tomorrow will do."

"BECCA, ARE YOU ready? It's five o'clock, so it's time," Kat said.

Staring at herself in the floor-to-ceiling mirror in the bridal room at the inn, Becca nodded. One by one, her friends formed a tight circle behind her. Kat, one of the bravest, fiercest women she knew. Emilie, one of the strongest and most generous. Sara, one of the most courageous and certainly the most resilient. Jenna, one of the most compassionate, with so much passion for life that she'd helped a broken man rediscover that within himself again.

How lucky was Becca to be surrounded by such extraordinary women? The only one missing was her own mother, and a little part of Becca's heart ached that her parents weren't there to see everything that she and Charlie had become. But that just proved that you had to love and cherish the ones you cared about while they were in your life and never waste a single minute.

"You look gorgeous," Sara said.

"We're all fucking hot," Kat said, making them all laugh.

"We are pretty stunning," Becca said. The gowns, the flowers in their hands and in their hair, the happiness radiating out from every one of their faces. "And I'm ready."

"Let me make sure the coast is clear. My brother has been a total crazy man about not seeing you." Kat winked at her as she made for the door. Becca hadn't seen Nick since they'd departed at noon for the salon. Truth be told, she was at her limit of missing him, too. "Okay, we're good."

They moved out into the main space, where Becca found Charlie waiting for her. The look he gave her was full of pride and affection.

"Are you feeling okay?" she asked him.

"Great," Charlie said. "I'm about to witness my favorite person on earth getting everything she ever wanted. How could I be anything but great?"

"I love you, Charlie," she said, gently hugging him.

"Bridesmaids, it's time to march," Sonya said. The lady had seemed a little rattled when they'd first arrived, but she'd really gone above and beyond in putting Becca at ease. But if Becca was honest, she didn't feel scarred by what had transpired there the day before. She felt freed.

One by one, her friends made their way to the dais at the far end of the courtyard.

"And now it's your turn," Sonya said as the music transitioned to the wedding march. "Congratulations, Becca."

"Thank you," she said as she slipped her arm through Charlie's good one. They stepped through the door and out into the evening sunlight. "I want this for you someday, Charlie. This happiness, this belonging. You deserve it."

He smiled. "I want it, too. And for the first time in my life, I believe I can have it."

"Jeremy is amazing," she said, giving him a little nudge with her elbow.

"Jeremy is everything," Charlie whispered as they neared the back row of chairs. The happiness in the words filled Becca's heart up to overflowing.

The audience all stood. It wasn't a huge gathering—a

handful of Nick's friends from various stages of his life, some of Becca's hospital colleagues and spouses, friends they'd made along the course of the investigation—Detective Vance, Walter and Louis Jackson, Chen. Ike and Jess, who worked at Hard Ink Tattoo, sat to the far side holding Eileen by her leash—the puppy wore a collar with wedding bells hanging off it and a veil that ran down her back. And to top it off, nearly twenty members of the Raven Riders Motorcycle Club had come, some with dates, some without. Before all this, Becca had never before met a person in a motorcycle club, but without them, Nick and his teammates would never have been able to win all the fights that had ultimately allowed the guys to clear their names.

And finally put the past to rest.

Becca was looking forward to getting to know the Ravens now that all the fighting was behind them.

Looking up, Becca found Nick straight ahead of her, looking as sexy as she'd *ever* seen him. His dress uniform highlighted the strong width of his shoulders and the trim leanness of his waist. Metals hanging on one side of his chest spoke of a man of honor, loyalty, bravery, and so much more. But what she most noticed was the expression on his face. Total, abject, unrestrained love, unconditional devotion, incredible respect.

If you had those things with the person walking through life with you, what more could you possibly want? Becca certainly didn't know.

As she got closer, she could see the men standing up

for Nick, standing by his side. Jeremy, who lived life with more pure delight than anyone she knew. Shane, within whom a fire to help and secure justice for others burned so bright. Marz, who was the most positive, loyal person she'd ever known. Easy, who would do anything for anyone, and who was one of the strongest people she'd ever met in her life, even if he didn't yet know it. And Beckett, fierce and self-sacrificing, the quintessential good guy hiding under a gruff exterior. She loved that about him. She loved all of them.

On a table in front of the men stood seven framed photographs. Her father and the six men from their A-team who hadn't survived that ambush on a dusty road in Afghanistan. They were all together again. Just as it should be.

Finally, she and Charlie reached the front. The chaplain asked, "Who presents this woman to be married to this man?"

"I do," Charlie said. He kissed her on the cheek, then turned to take a seat.

Except before he could do so, Kat came down the two brick steps, grabbed his hand, and led him to stand with her. "You should be here, too," she said.

It was the first moment all day that made Becca have to fight back tears.

Nick stepped forward and took her hand, and the glassiness in his eyes hammered the next nail into her effort to make it through the ceremony without smearing her makeup. As he guided her up the steps, he whispered,

"I love you, Becca. I am absolutely the luckiest man alive."

"I love you, too, Nick. Always and forever," she whispered back.

And as they exchanged their vows and claimed one another with their rings and confirmed their commitment in front of everyone they loved, Becca knew this was what happily ever after felt like.

"Ladies and gentlemen," the chaplain called out when they'd said everything that needed to be said, "may I present the new mister and missus Nick and Becca Rixey. You may seal your union with a kiss."

As applause erupted, Nick slid his big hand behind her neck and slowly pulled her in. The kiss was deep and soulful and claiming, full of love and heat, the kind of kiss she would remember as an old lady, the kind of kiss that would make her remember that, once, she'd really lived.

But living was what she was all about now. And *this kiss* was what their happily ever after was going to feel like all the time. Full of life and passion and love.

And if they ran into some hard times along the way, they'd fight through them together. Side by side. Surrounded by their friends.

After all, hard ever afters were good, too.

Because hard is good.

Acknowledgments

THANK YOU FIRST and foremost to Amanda Bergeron, my amazing editor at Avon, for thinking this book was as fun an idea as I did, and for agreeing to the title that still makes me chuckle! Working with you has been one of the greatest pleasures of my career, and I adore that you love all these guys as much as I do. Thanks also to my agent, Kevan Lyon, for loving the idea of this book, and to KP Simmons for everything you did to make the incredible invitations and announcements that we used during the voting for the book's couple.

I also want to thank all the readers who participated in the vote to determine which couple the book would feature. I adored how many of you wanted it to be about *all* the couples, and I hope the book gave you enough of a follow-up with everyone to whet your whistle! It was *so* much fun writing these characters again, and I can't thank you enough for giving me a reason to dive back into the Hard Ink world.

Thanks to writing friends Lea Nolan, Christi Barth, and Stephanie Dray, who helped me think through the suspense plotline of the story and just generally provide support and encouragement. You all are the best!

This book had a ton of support from readers and bloggers along the way—first with the voting, then with the cover reveal, and finally with the release. I couldn't do what I love so much without your support, so THANK YOU to the amazing blogging community that has turned out so often to support the Hard Ink books and me more generally. You guys rock so hard!

Thank you to my husband and daughters for dealing with mom on deadline again! Your support and encouragement means the world! Finally, thank you to the readers who take my characters into their hearts and allow them to tell their stories over and over again. Read hard, dear readers, always and forever.

LK

Get ready to meet
The Raven Riders
Coming May 2016

RIDE HARD

Brotherhood. Club. Family.
They live and ride by their own rules.
These are the Raven Riders . . .

Raven Riders Motorcycle Club president Dare Kenyon
rides hard and values loyalty above all else. He'll do anything to protect the brotherhood of bikers—the only
family he's got—as well as those who can't defend themselves. So when mistrustful Haven Randall lands on the
club's doorstep scared that she's being hunted, Dare takes
her in, swears to keep her safe, and pushes to learn the
secrets overshadowing her pretty smile.

Haven fled from years of abuse at the hands of her
criminal father and is suspicious of any man's promises,
including those of the darkly sexy and overwhelmingly
intense Ravens leader. But as the powerful attraction

between them flares to life, Dare pushes her boundaries and tempts her to want things she never thought she could.

The past never dies without a fight, but Dare Kenyon's never backed down before. . . .

Keep reading for a first look . . .

Chapter One

To say that Haven Randall's escape plans were not going as she'd hoped was quite possibly the understatement of the century. Especially since she wasn't at all sure her current situation was any better than the one she'd run from three weeks before.

But today could be the day she found that out for sure.

Staring out the window through the slats of the blinds, Haven watched as another group of motorcycles roared into the parking lot below. They'd been coming in groups of four or five for the past hour or so. And, *God*, there were a lot of them. Not surprising, since she was currently holed up at the compound of the Raven Riders Motorcycle Club. A shiver raced over her skin.

"Don't worry," Haven's friend Cora Campbell said. Sitting on the bed, back against the wall, her choppy, shoulder-length blond hair twisted up in a messy bun, Cora gave Haven a reassuring smile.

"I don't know what I'd do without you," Haven said. And it was the truth. Without Cora's bravery, encouragement, and fearless you-only-live-once attitude, Haven never would've put her longtime pipe dream of escaping from her father's house into action. Of course, those actions had landed her here, among a bunch of strange bikers of questionable character and intent, and Haven didn't know what to make of that. Yet.

But it had to be better than what would've happened if she'd stayed in Georgia. She had to believe that. *Had to*.

"Well, you won't ever have to find out," Cora said, flipping through an old gossip magazine that had been on the nightstand. "Because you're stuck with me."

"I wouldn't want to be stuck with anyone else," Haven said in a quiet voice.

Outside, the late-day sun gleamed off the steel and chrome of the motorcycles slowly but surely filling the lot. The bass beat of rock music suddenly drummed against the floor of their room. Now the Ravens' clubhouse, the building where they'd been staying for just over two weeks now had apparently once been an old mountain inn. Their rooms were on the second floor, where guests used to stay, and though Cora had been more adventurous, Haven had stayed in her room as much as possible since they'd arrived. And that was while the majority of the guys had been away from their compound on some sort of club business.

Men's laughter boomed from downstairs.

Haven hugged herself as another group of bikers tore into the lot. "There are so many of them."

Cora tossed the magazine aside and climbed off the bed. She was wearing a plain gray tank top and a pair of cutoff shorts that Bunny, an older lady who was married to one of the Ravens, had lent her. Haven's baggy white T-shirt and loose khaki cargo pants were borrowed, too. They'd run away with a few articles of clothes and cash that Haven had stolen from her father, but they'd lost all of that—and their only vehicle—two weeks ago. She and Cora literally had nothing of their own in the whole world.

Haven's belly tossed. Being totally dependent on anyone else was the last thing she wanted. She was too familiar with all the ways that could be used against her to make her do things she didn't want to do.

Standing next to her at the window, Cora said, "We're not prisoners here, Haven. We're their guests. Remember what Ike said."

Haven nodded. "I know." She hadn't forgotten. Ike Young was the member of the Ravens who had brought them there, who'd told them they were welcome to stay as long as they needed to, who said that no one would give them any trouble. Who said the Ravens helped people like them all the time.

People like them.

So, people like someone who'd grown up as the daughter of the head of a criminal organization? Someone who'd been homeschooled starting in tenth grade so her father could control her every move—and make sure she never saw her first and only boyfriend again? Someone whose father used her for a maid and a cook and planned to barter her off in a forced marriage to another crime family to cement an alliance? Someone who, after managing a middle-of-the-night escape, ended up being captured by a drug-dealing gang seven hundred miles away—a gang that had apparently received notice of a reward for capture from her father? Someone who was then rescued by soldiers and bikers at war with that gang?

Because that was Haven's reality, and she really doubted the Ravens had helped people like her before. Or, at least, she hoped not. Because she wouldn't wish the life she'd lived so far on her worst enemy.

And, *God,* was it possible her father was still looking for her? Was it possible that others, motivated by that reward, were hunting her, too? Her stomach got a sour, wiggly feeling that left her feeling nauseous.

"I'm okay," she said, giving Cora another smile. "Really." Maybe if she kept reassuring Cora of that, she'd begin to believe it herself.

"Listen, it's almost seven. Bunny said there'd be a big celebratory dinner tonight to welcome everyone back. Let's go down." Cora's bright green eyes were filled with so much enthusiasm and excitement.

Haven hated nothing more than disappointing her friend—her *only* friend, really. The only one who hadn't given up on her when Haven had been forced to drop out of school in tenth grade. Cora's father occasionally worked for Haven's, which had paved the way for Cora to be allowed to visit and even sleep over. Haven had lived for those visits, especially when her father's tight control hadn't let up even after she'd turned eighteen. Or twenty-one.

"I don't know, Cora. Can you just bring me some food later?" Haven asked, dubious that her appetite was going to rebound but knowing Cora liked taking care of her, running interference for her, protecting her. Despite how tense things had been at her father's house, Cora had slept over more and more in the time before they'd finally run. Because she'd known it had cheered Haven up so much. "I'm not hungry right now anyway."

"Oh," Cora said. "You know what? I'm not that hungry, either. I'll just wait." Her stomach growled. Loudly.

Haven stared at her, and they both chuckled. "Just go," Haven said. "Don't stay here because I'm too chicken to be around a bunch of strangers. Really. I'm so used to being alone. You know I don't mind."

Cora frowned. "That's exactly why I don't like leaving you."

"I'll feel bad if you stay. Go. Eat, visit, and meet everybody. Maybe . . . maybe I'll come down later," she said. Yeah. Maybe after the dinner was over, she could sneak down to the kitchen and help Bunny clean up. That might allow her to get a feel for some of the club members without being right in the middle of them, without feeling like she was under a microscope with everyone looking at her and wondering about her.

Grasping her hand, Cora's gaze narrowed. "Are you sure? You know I don't mind hanging out."

"Totally sure." Besides, Haven couldn't help but feel like she held Cora back. Cora was adventurous and outgoing and pretty much down for anything at any time, which was one of the main reasons Haven was here and not in

Georgia married to a horrible stranger. But now Cora was on the run, too, though every time Haven expressed guilt about that, Cora told her it was better than waitressing at the truck stop back home and watching her father drink too much. "I might actually take a nap anyway. I didn't sleep great last night . . ." Because Bunny had told them all the bikers would be returning to the club today.

Cora just nodded. She didn't have to ask Haven to explain. She knew her too well. "Okay, well, I'll bring food back later. But come down if you think you can. Even for a few minutes. Okay?"

"Yup." Haven sat on the edge of the bed and threw a wave when Cora looked back over her shoulder. The door clicked shut behind her friend. On a huff, Haven flopped backwards against the hard mattress. Why couldn't she be more like Cora? Or, at least, more normal?

Because what did gaining her freedom mean if she was too scared to ever actually live?

DARE KENYON SHOULD'VE been happy—or at least content. The huge fight his club had joined with the team of Special Forces Army veterans operating out of Baltimore's Hard Ink Tattoo was over, those who'd been responsible for killing two of his brothers were either dead or in custody, and all Dare's people were here at the compound, safe and sound and partying it up like tomorrow might never come.

Which made sense, since today was all anyone was ever guaranteed to get.

Standing at the far end of the carved wooden bar in the club's big rec room, Dare contemplated the tumbler of whiskey in his hand. Tilting it from side to side, he watched the amber liquid flow around the ice, the dim lighting reflecting off the facets in the cut glass. Around him, his brothers busted out in laughter as rock music filled the room with a pulsing beat. Couples danced and drank and groped. In shadowy corners here and there, people were pairing up, making out, getting hot enough to find a room upstairs. Hell, some of them didn't mind witnesses, either.

Finally, Dare tossed back a gulp of whiskey, savoring the biting heat as it seared down his throat.

"Hey, Dare." A woman with curly blond hair, a deep V-neck, and huge heels stepped up to the counter beside him. She ordered a drink from Blake, one of the prospects working the bar tonight, then turned her big smile and a generous eyeful of her cleavage toward Dare.

"Carly," he said, giving her a nod and already considering whether he was interested in what she no doubt was about to offer. He'd been with her a few times, though not much lately, since it had become more and more clear she was holding out hope to be his Old Lady.

"I'm sure glad you all are back," she said, sidling closer until she was leaning against him, her breasts against his arm, her hand rubbing his back. She was pretty, but she was also a sweet thing, the club's nickname for the attractive women who partied at the clubhouse and hung out at their track on race nights, seeking attention from and offering themselves to the brothers. Dare didn't mind having friends like Carly in the community, but he knew her interest was as much in being a part of the MC scene as it was in him. At thirty-seven, he wasn't sure he was ever going to settle down with one woman, but if he did, it certainly wasn't going to be with someone half his brothers had enjoyed, too.

And, anyway, he wasn't looking.

Dare just nodded to Carly as she pressed her way in closer until the whole front of her was tight against his side. Her hands wandered to his chest, his ass, his dick. Her lips ghosted over his cheek. "I missed you." Her hand squeezed his growing erection through his jeans. "Missed you a lot."

"Did you, now?" he said, taking another swig of Jack. The friction of her hand was luring him out of his head, out from under the strain of being responsible for so many people. It was an honor, one he'd built his life around, but he felt the weight of it some days more than others. Losing Harvey and Creed almost two weeks before, he felt that weight like a motherfucker. Hell if every new loss in his life didn't whip up his guilt from the first two . . .

Sonofabitch.

Carly combed her fingers through the length of his brown hair, pushing it back off his face so she could whisper into his ear. "I did. Would you like me to show you how much?" Her fingers slowly worked at his zipper, tugging him from his thoughts.

Exactly what he needed. "What is it you have in mind?" He peered down at her, really appreciating the easy, lighthearted expression on her face. Nothing too deep, nothing too heavy, but full of life all the same.

Her fingers undid the button on his jeans and slipped in against his skin, finding and palming his now rigid cock. Fuck, that felt good. Warm and tight and full of promise.

Smiling, Carly slid herself in front of Dare, pinning her body between his and the hard wooden counter. Her eyes were full of heat and need. "I could drop to my knees right here. Suck you off. Let you fuck my face. Or we could go upstairs, baby. Whatever you want." With the hand not stroking him, she wrapped an arm around his neck, her fingers playing with the long strands of his hair. "You seem . . . tense, upset. Let me make you feel better?"

And now, on top of everything else, he had a warm, willing woman wanting to make him forget all his troubles. So, yeah, he should've been content.

Dare emptied his glass and slammed it down on the counter. Fuck it. Grasping her face in his hand, he trailed his thumb over her bottom lip, stroking, dipping inside so she could suck on his flesh. "Always did love that mouth," he said.

She grinned around his thumb and nodded, then she slowly slid down his body.

Dare closed his eyes, wanting nothing more than to lose himself in the moment, the sensation, the physical. But his gut wouldn't stop telling him that some part of their recent troubles were going to come back and bite them in the ass. The past had a way of doing that. Which was why Dare always kept one eye trained over his shoulder. But this particular past was only days old and way bigger than their typical fights. Along with the SpecOps team operating out of Hard Ink, the Ravens had played a role in taking down longtime enemies and Baltimore's biggest heroin dealers—the Church Gang. In the process, they'd exposed an international drug smuggling conspiracy involving a team of former soldiers turned hired mercenaries and at least one three-star, active-duty general. The Ravens had initially come into the fight as hired help, but they'd soon taken up the cause as their own when Harvey and Creed had been killed.

Given all that, Dare had a really fucking hard time believing the dust would just settle and life would go back to normal without any blowback.

As Carly got into a crouched position at his feet, Dare opened his eyes and tried to shake away all the churn and burn in his head. But then his gaze snagged on a girl in the doorway across the room. Clarity stole over him, pushing away the fog of lust and the haze of troubled thoughts. The girl had the longest blond hair he'd ever seen, like some fairy-tale princess, or a fucking angel. Pale, small, almost too beautiful to look at. She stood out so starkly that it was almost as if she glowed in the dim room. Like a beacon. Bright and shiny and new.

One of these things is not like the other. And it was the timid beauty wearing too-big clothes and no makeup, hovering on the edge of the room.

And Dare wasn't the only man who noticed.

THE WORLD OF HARD INK
Don't miss the rest of
New York Times bestselling author
Laura Kaye's breathtakingly
thrilling Hard Ink series!

HARD AS IT GETS

Tall, dark, and lethal . . .

Trouble just walked into Nicholas Rixey's tattoo parlor. Becca Merritt is warm, sexy, wholesome—pure temptation to a very jaded Nick. He's left his military life behind to become co-owner of Hard Ink Tattoo, but Becca is his ex-commander's daughter. Loyalty won't let him turn her away. Lust has plenty to do with it, too.

With her brother presumed kidnapped, Becca needs Nick. She just wasn't expecting to want him so much. As their investigation turns into all-out war with an organized crime ring, only Nick can protect her. And only Becca can heal the scars no one else sees.

Desire is the easy part. Love is as hard as it gets. Good thing Nick is always up for a challenge . . .

Available Now

HARD AS YOU CAN

Ever since hard-bodied, drop-dead-charming Shane Mc-Callan strolled into the dance club where Crystal Dean works, he's shown a knack for getting beneath her defenses. For her little sister's sake, Crystal can't get too close. Until her job and Shane's mission intersect, and he reveals talents that go deeper than she could have guessed.

Shane would never turn his back on a friend in need, especially a former Special Forces teammate running a dangerous, off-the-books operation. Nor can he walk away from Crystal. The gorgeous waitress is hiding secrets she doesn't want him to uncover. Too bad. He's exactly the man she needs to protect her sister, her life, and her heart. All he has to do is convince her that when something feels this good, you hold on as hard as you can—and never let go.

Available Now

HARD TO HOLD ON TO

Edward "Easy" Cantrell knows better than most the pain of not being able to save those he loves—which is why he is not going to let Jenna Dean out of his sight. He may have just met her, but Jenna's the first person to make him feel alive since that devastating day in the desert more than a year ago.

Jenna has never met anyone like Easy. She can't describe how he makes her feel—and not just because he saved her life. No, the stirrings inside her reach far beyond gratitude.

As the pair are thrust together while chaos reigns around them, they both know one thing: the things in life most worth having are the hardest to hold on to.

Available Now

HARD TO COME BY

Caught between desire and loyalty . . .

Derek DiMarzio would do anything for the members of his disgraced Special Forces team—sacrifice his body, help a former teammate with a covert operation to restore their honor, and even go behind enemy lines. He just never expected to want the beautiful woman he found there.

When a sexy stranger asks questions about her brother, Emilie Garza is torn between loyalty to the brother she once idolized and fear of the war-changed man he's become. Derek's easy smile and quiet strength tempt Emilie to open up, igniting the desire between them and leading Derek to crave a woman he shouldn't trust.

As the team's investigation reveals how powerful their enemies are, Derek and Emilie must prove where their loyalties lie before hearts are broken and lives are lost. Because love is too hard to come by to let slip away . . .

Available Now

HARD TO BE GOOD

Hard Ink Tattoo owner Jeremy Rixey has taken on his brother's stateside fight against the forces that nearly killed Nick and his Special Forces team a year before. Now, Jeremy's whole world has been turned upside down—not the least of which by a brilliant, quiet blond man who tempts Jeremy to settle down for the first time ever.

Recent kidnapping victim Charlie Merritt has always been better with computers than people, so when he's drawn into the SF team's investigation of his army colonel father's corruption, he's surprised to find acceptance and friendship—especially since his father never accepted who Charlie was. Even more surprising is the heated tension Charlie feels with sexy, tattooed Jeremy, Charlie's opposite in almost every way.

With tragedy and chaos all around them, temptation flashes hot, and Jeremy and Charlie can't help but wonder why they're trying so hard to be good . . .

Available Now

HARD TO LET GO

Beckett Murda hates to dwell on the past. But his investigation into the ambush that killed half his Special Forces team and ended his Army career gives him little choice. Just when his team learns how powerful their enemies are, hard-ass Beckett encounters his biggest complication yet—a seductive, feisty Katherine Rixey.

A tough, stubborn prosecutor, Kat visits her brothers' Hard Ink Tattoo shop following a bad break-up—and finds herself staring down the barrel of a stranger's gun. Beckett is hard-bodied and sexy as hell, but he's also the most infuriating man ever. Worse, Kat's brothers are at war with the criminals her office is investigating. When Kat joins the fight, she lands straight in Beckett's sights . . . and in his arms. Not to mention their enemies' crosshairs.

Now Beckett and Kat must set aside their differences to work together, because the only thing sweeter than justice is finding love and never letting go.

Available Now

HARD AS STEEL

After identifying her employer's dangerous enemies, Jessica Jakes takes refuge at the compound of the Raven Riders Motorcycle Club. Fellow Hard Ink tattooist and Raven leader Ike Young promises to keep Jess safe for as long as it takes, which would be perfect if his close, personal, round-the-clock protection didn't make it so hard to hide just how much she wants him—and always has.

Ike Young loved and lost a woman in trouble once before. The last thing he needs is alone time with the sexiest and feistiest woman he's ever known, one he's purposely kept at a distance for years. Now, Ike's not sure he can keep his hands or his heart to himself—or that he even wants to anymore. And that means he has to do whatever it takes to hold on to Jess forever.

Available Now

HARD EVER AFTER

After a long battle to discover the truth, the men and women of Hard Ink have a lot to celebrate, especially the wedding of two of their own—Nick Rixey and Becca Merritt—whose hard-fought love deserves a happy ending.

As Nick and the team shift from crisis mode to building their new security consulting firm, Becca heads back to work at the ER. But amid the everyday chaos of their demanding jobs and upcoming nuptials, an old menace they thought was long gone reemerges, threatening the peace they've only just found.

Now, for one last time, Nick and Becca must fight for their always and forever, because they know that when true love overcomes all the odds, it lasts hard ever after.

Available Now

HARD TO SERVE

To protect and serve is all Detective Kyler Vance ever wanted to do, so when Internal Affairs investigates him as part of the new police commissioner's bid to oust corruption, everything is on the line. Which makes meeting a smart, gorgeous submissive at an exclusive play club the perfect distraction . . .

The director of the city's hottest art gallery, Mia Breslin's career is golden. Now if only she could find a man to dominate her nights and set her body—and her heart—on fire. When a scorching scene with a hard-bodied, brooding Dom at Blasphemy promises just that, Mia is lured to serve Kyler again and again.

As their relationship burns hotter, Kyler runs into Mia at work and learns that he's been dominating the daughter of the hard-ass boss who has it in for him. Now Kyler must choose between life-long duty and forbidden desire before Mia finds another who's not so hard to serve.

Coming June 2016

About the Author

LAURA KAYE is the *New York Times* and *USA Today* bestselling author of over twenty books in contemporary romance and romantic suspense, including *Hard As You Can*, winner of the RT Reviewers' Choice Award for Best Romantic Suspense of 2014, and *Hard to Let Go*, nominated for the 2015 RT Award. Laura grew up amid family lore involving angels, ghosts, and evil-eye curses, cementing her lifelong fascination with storytelling and the supernatural. A former college history professor, Laura also writes historical women's fiction as Laura Kamoie. Laura lives in Maryland with her husband, two daughters, and cute-but-bad dog, and appreciates her view of the Chesapeake Bay every day. Learn more at www.LauraKayeAuthor.com.

Discover great authors, exclusive offers, and more at hc.com.

About the Author

LAURA KAYE is the *New York Times* and *USA Today* bestselling author of over twenty books in contemporary romance and romantic suspense, including *Hard As You Fall*, winner of the RT Reviewers' Choice Award for Best Erotic Romance Suspense of 2014, and *Hard to Let Go*, nominated for the 2015 RT Award. Laura grew up in a... and family lore involving angels, ghosts, and evil-eye curses, cementing her lifelong fascination with story-telling and the supernatural. A former college history professor, Laura also writes historical women's fiction as Laura Kamoie. Laura lives in Maryland with her husband, two daughters, and cute but bad dog, and appreciates her view of the Chesapeake Bay every day. Learn more at www.laurakayeauthor.com.

Give in to your Impulses . . .
Continue reading for excerpts from
our newest Avon Impulse books.
Available now wherever ebooks are sold.

EVERYTHING SHE WANTED
BOOK FIVE: THE HUNTED SERIES
by Jennifer Ryan

WHEN WE KISS
RIBBON RIDGE BOOK FIVE
by Darcy Burke

An Excerpt from

EVERYTHING SHE WANTED
Book Five: The Hunted Series
By Jennifer Ryan

Ben Knight has spent his life protecting those
in need and helping abused women escape their
terrible circumstances. He'll stop at nothing
to save the lives of his clients, especially the
hauntingly beautiful Kate Morrison, a woman
threatened by a man whose wealth allows him to
get away with everything—including murder.

Ben pulled in behind several police cars nearly thirty minutes later, their red and blue lights flashing. He turned off the car's engine and sat staring up at the massive house. Morgan's prediction played in his mind. This late at night, the woman meant for him had to be in that house. He hoped she wasn't the dead woman Detective Raynott called him about.

Evan Faraday hit Ben's radar when Detective Raynott caught the case of a man found beaten to death in an alley after gambling with some guys in the bar, including Evan. That man was the son of one of his Haven House clients. Ben stepped in as a legal advocate for the family. The guy was only trying to scrape together extra money for his mother and sister. Evan played cards with the guy, but Raynott couldn't link him to the murder. Not with any actual evidence, but the circumstantial kind added up to Evan drunk and pissed off about losing to the guy. Evan killed him; they just couldn't prove it.

More recently, Evan got into another bar fight. Donald Faraday paid off the guy with a heavy heart. He knew what and who his son was, but that didn't stop him from getting Evan out of trouble. Again.

Detective Raynott caught that case too. Ben asked the detective to call him if Evan got in trouble again. Ben wanted to take the selfish, smart-mouthed prick down. Then came the DUI arrest. Now he'd killed again.

Ben got out of the car, tucked in his shirt, and straightened his tie.

"What am I doing?" He was at a murder scene, not meeting a date for drinks and dinner.

But she was in there. He knew it. Anticipated it. And hoped he wasn't a fool for believing in Morgan.

The anticipation and hope swamping his system surprised him more than a little. He hadn't realized how much he wanted a woman in his life. Not just any woman, but the right woman.

"I'm sorry, sir, this is an active crime scene. Law enforcement only," the officer guarding the police line said. Ben noted the neighbors' interest. They lined the street, whispering to each other and staring at him. Some in their bathrobes, others in lounge clothes. This late at night the sirens got most of them up out of their beds. In this neighborhood, a murder was the last thing they expected.

"My name is Ben Knight. Detective Raynott called and asked me to come."

The officer held the tape up for him to pass. "He's in the living room. Give your name to the officer at the door."

Ben did and stepped into the elegant home and surveyed the officers and crime scene techs working the scene at the back of the house and what looked like the entrance to the kitchen. He spotted Detective Raynott standing over a woman with long brown wavy hair, a baby sleeping in a car seat at her feet. With her back to him, he couldn't see her face, but something about her seemed familiar. A strange tug pulled him toward her.

"Ben, you made it. Thanks for coming," Detective Raynott said, waving him forward.

"Anything to nail Evan Faraday and see him behind bars."

The woman turned and raised her face to look up at him. He stopped midstride and stared into her beautiful blue eyes. Like a deep lake, the soft outer color darkened toward the center. "Kate?"

He never expected her. Morgan had been right though—they'd shared a moment at a wedding reception for a mutual friend and colleague. That had been more than a year ago now. They sat at the same table and talked, mostly about work and how out of place they felt at the event, made even more uncomfortable when they realized they were seated at a table full of singles and the bride had arranged them as couples, playing matchmaker. They shared some laughs and danced, deciding to make the awkward situation fun. They fell under the spell—the music, champagne, the celebration of love—and Ben enjoyed himself more that night than any other date. He kissed her right there on the dance floor during a particularly slow, sweet song. He remembered it perfectly. The way she stared up at him with those blue eyes. The way her mouth parted slightly as she exhaled and he leaned in. The softness of her lips against his. The way she gave in to the kiss with a soft sigh. The tremble that rocked his body and hers when the sparks flew and sizzled through his system.

The startled look on her face when he pulled back just enough to see the desire flaming in her eyes. A split second later she bolted for the door.

Jennifer Ryan

He went after her, but didn't find her. She didn't answer his calls over the next two days. He still didn't know if he'd overstepped, done something wrong, or simply scared her.

"Ben." Her soft voice, filled with surprise, startled him out of his thoughts. "What are you doing here?" Her sad eyes narrowed on him.

An Excerpt from

WHEN WE KISS
Ribbon Ridge Book Five
By Darcy Burke

In the fifth novel in the Ribbon Ridge series, thrill-seeker Liam Archer will try anything once—except falling in love—but what happens when the one woman whose kiss is better than any adrenaline high puts an end to their no-strings fling?

Aubrey Tallinger finished drying her hands and set the towel down. Lifting her head, she caught her reflection in the mirror. Her hazel eyes stared back at her and seemed to ask what she was doing dawdling in the bathroom when a perfectly lovely wedding reception was going on.

Isn't it obvious? I'm avoiding Liam.

She was proud of herself tonight. She'd done a good job of ignoring the one person who always seemed to command her attention: Liam Archer. It helped to have a date along. A date she should get back to.

She took a deep breath and opened the door. Liam stood on the other side of the threshold.

He grabbed her hand and dragged her to the left through a doorway. He let go of her to close the door then stood in front of it, his blue-gray eyes narrowed. "Who's the loser?"

Aubrey registered that they were in a sitting room attached to his parents' bedroom. She wanted to turn and look at the sun setting over the garden through the back windows, but couldn't tear her eyes from Liam. Dressed in a crisp black suit with a natty, striped tie, he was the sexiest best man she'd ever seen. His dark wavy hair was perfectly styled and, as usual, she had an almost irrepressible urge to mess it up.

She tensed as she forced herself to present a cool demeanor. "I introduced you to him at the church."

"Yes, Stuart the Accountant. But why did you bring him in the first place?"

She cocked her head and gave him a sarcastic stare. "Was I supposed to wait for you to ask me? You don't take me on *dates*, Liam. You never have." The dinner he'd surprised her with at her house when he'd been home for the long Thanksgiving weekend didn't count. Dates were *public*.

He frowned, and she was shocked when he didn't fire a snappy comeback. "I might've, actually."

Ha! She'd believe that when she saw it. "Too late. I told you at New Year's that our little . . . *thing* was done."

"It wasn't a *thing*."

"No, I think you're right. It was a series of convenient hook-ups, and they are no longer convenient to me."

She called them hook-ups, but they'd been more than that. Every time they were together, she'd felt as though they'd connected on some sort of intimate level that went beyond just sex. But that was stupid. While she'd come to know him at least a little bit, they hadn't spent enough day-to-day time together to allow anything meaningful to spark. Except for Labor Day weekend. They'd spent the better part of four days in each other's company, and it had been bliss. They'd laughed, they'd danced, they'd talked. And yes, they'd had a lot of sex. The physical aspect of their connection was so far the most powerful.

He prowled toward her, like a jungle cat on the hunt. She had no intention of being his prey. Nor did she want to run. She stiffened her spine and crossed her arms over her chest.

Meager protection when she knew just how dangerous his weapons of mass seduction could be.

"Come on, they were a little more than hook-ups. We *planned* to hang out over Labor Day."

That was true, but they'd both been going to the Dave Matthews Band concerts up in central Washington anyway. It wasn't like they'd formulated and executed the trip together.

He stopped in front of her, his lips curving up. "And you have to admit it was pretty great."

Incredible. Right up to the point when she'd suggested they see each other again soon. He'd said, "Sure, I always call you up when I'm in town."

Like she was a convenience. And there was that word again. She didn't want to be anyone's hook-up girl. She'd quashed her burgeoning feelings, but it had maybe been too late. She'd already been crazy infatuated with him. So much so that when she'd seen him at Thanksgiving, she'd allowed herself to be the convenience she didn't want to be.

But no more.

She gave him an arch look. "So it was a great weekend. You still can't argue it was more than a hook-up. I walked away from that without knowing when—or if—I'd see you again."

He frowned at her. "That's absurd. You're our attorney. Of course you'd see me again."

Was he being purposely obnoxious?

He put his hands on his hips. "I suppose you're going to tell me Thanksgiving was just a hook-up, too? I brought you dinner."

After they'd flirted all day at a winery event they'd just happened to meet at. She'd accepted his sister Tori's invitation to attend without realizing Liam would be there. Wait, had he known? "Did you know I would be at the winery that day?"

He arched a brow. "Who do you think suggested we invite you?"

Damn it. She didn't want to know that. "Now you tell me," she muttered.

He flashed her a grin. "Am I wearing you down?"